THE HEALER AND THE DRAGON

THE HEALER AND THE DRAGON

THE CURSED WYRM COURT™
BOOK ONE

RIVER TATUM

MICHAEL ANDERLE

DON'T MISS OUR NEW RELEASES

Join the Florid Romance email list to be notified of new releases and special promotions (which happen often) by following this link:

https://floridromance.lmbpn.com/about/sign-up-for-our-newsletter/

Published by Florid Romance
an imprint of LMBPN Publishing
2375 E. Tropicana Avenue, Suite 8-305
Las Vegas, Nevada 89119 USA

Version 1.00, May 2025
eBook ISBN: 979-8-89354-785-6
Print ISBN: 979-8-89354-786-3

CHAPTER

ONE

Nyra Vexlin knelt on the cobblestones of the Redwick village square, sweat trickling down her face as she concentrated. Shouts and chatter rippled around her, but she kept her attention fixed on the man before her. His skin was gray-tinged and damp with fever. Dozens of villagers stood at a distance, murmuring soft words of worry, because everyone knew the affliction he had: Fogrot. It was a dreaded magical disease, a curse, really, that left its victims thrashing in near-delirium, a creeping malaise that turned skin cold and tongues useless.

Nyra's patient trembled as he lay on a patchy quilt spread over the ground beneath him. His shallow breaths made her worry his lungs were already compromised. Even so, she pressed her palm gently on his chest. The tension in his muscles made her heart twist.

"I think your family got you here just in time," she said softly, although she did not know if he could hear. The man moaned in pain. His wife, kneeling beside him, oppo-

1

site Nyra, had red-rimmed eyes from crying. A child clutched the woman's skirt and stared at Nyra with a tearful expression that asked the healer to save her daddy. That child's face made Nyra's heart pound with determination.

Behind them, the mayor of the Redwick Village stood with two strangers. Their regal attire set them apart from the villagers' simpler clothes. One had a lean build and keen, dark eyes. The other was broader in the shoulders, with a silver chain glinting across a finely embroidered jacket. Together, they had the air of quiet authority and more money than Nyra would likely see in ten lifetimes. Nearby, a brave cluster of the village's more curious residents craned their necks to see what these strangers wanted and why they had come. But for the moment, most of the villagers' focus remained with Nyra, who prepared to heal the cursed man.

She uncorked a small glass vial and swirled the cool liquid inside. The pungent scent of herbs drifted into the stifling summer air. Moonpetal Tincture, gathered painstakingly over weeks of searching remote meadows by moonlight, might be enough to halt Fogrot's spread. At least, that was the hope.

Nyra leaned over the man, carefully tilting his jaw so he would not choke on the tincture as she poured it into his mouth. Then she dabbed a portion of it onto his forehead, as well, where it formed a faint trail of shimmering residue as it slid down the side of his head. She placed a trembling hand on his chest and took in a slow breath. She needed a few lines of incantation to help guide the magic through his bloodstream, to push the Fogrot out before it took full hold and drove him into madness. She closed her eyes and spoke, voice low and intense:

"By silver's gleam and moon's pale light,
Banish the fog and end this blight.
Let warmth flow free through mortal shell;
Heal the flesh and break this spell."

She felt her energy thrumming through her and into her patient. It coursed into the man's body, and she sensed the fog of the curse struggling to linger. The blue tint under his skin quivered and coiled like a living thing before the healing force began to suppress it. Gradually, the man's ragged breathing steadied.

He gave a sudden gasp. His eyes fluttered open, and the mottled patches on his skin began to recede, fading from a sickly blue-gray to a more natural pallor. A new hush fell over the crowd. Then relief broke the silence, and scattered applause mixed with cries of joy rose around them.

Nyra allowed herself a deeper breath as she pulled away. The man's wife burst into tears and clutched her husband's hand. The child, who had watched everything with tight-lipped concern, flung small arms around Nyra as if to anchor a passing angel. Nyra patted the child's back and offered a gentle smile.

"Thank you," whispered the wife, her voice trembling with emotion. "I want to pay but we do not have much." She pressed a single ducket into Nyra's palm, one tiny coin that likely represented a month's wages for them. Nyra swallowed hard at the gesture. The family's gratitude felt both humbling and bittersweet, and she hesitated before tucking the coin into the pouch at her waist.

Wiping the sweat from her brow, Nyra noted the mayor's footsteps approaching as the family helped their loved one to sit up. A few moments later, the man stood, testing his balance by holding his arms out in front of him like a toddler learning to walk. Satisfied he was stable, he smiled a wide, toothless grin and threw his arms out wide and laughed. The crowd laughed with him and cheered, as he kissed Nyra's hand and then was enveloped in the arms of his family.

Nyra turned to face the mayor. His thinning hair looked as though it had wilted in the heat, and lines of tension formed across his forehead. At his side stood the two strangers. They seemed to be studying her with an intensity that made her shift uncomfortably.

"Well done, Nyra," the mayor said. "Another life saved by your gifted hands." He paused, glancing over his shoulder at the two figures. "These gentlemen asked to observe your work. They come under the authority of King Vorian."

An uneasy ripple went through the remaining onlookers. The mention of the king reminded everyone of the vast difference between the humble village and the royal seat. Dressed in fine garments, the strangers stepped forward. The taller one bowed slightly, though it felt measured and deliberate.

"Allow me to introduce myself. I am Jori, and this is

Harmond," the taller man said. "We are part of King Vorian's privy council. The king has urgent business that concerns you."

Nyra's pulse fluttered at his words. She closed her medicine satchel with careful slowness. Usually, no one from the royal court took notice of her or her small corner of the kingdom. She nodded politely, though apprehension gripped her stomach.

Councilor Harmond folded his hands. His tone was smooth but carried an edge of tension. "We have heard of your healing skills. The afflicted man you just cured is proof that the rumors we have heard are not exaggerations." He studied Nyra as though assessing her potential.

"Fogrot isn't hard to heal, really." Nyra regarded the two men with distrust. Anyone from the king's court couldn't be trusted. They were all simply fat cats, she'd heard, feasting in their fortress castle while the rest of the country starved. The sooner she got rid of them, the better. "Just needs the right tincture and incantation. It's a stubborn malady, though. Sometimes, it just refuses to fade away."

"We need a healer for a dire case, far beyond any mundane disease you've cured before," Harmond replied. "This case is a special one."

"Special, indeed," Jori added.

Nyra glanced from Harmond to Jori. She caught a glimpse of the mayor, who seemed caught between pride for his village's talented healer and fear at what the king's men might demand. "I do what I must to help whoever is in need," she said.

The two councilors exchanged a look. Jori spoke quietly, "You have heard of Prince Rhezan, I assume?"

Nyra's mouth tightened. Of course she'd heard of the crown prince—the beast cloistered in the mountains, cursed and half-mad, if the whispers were true. A temper like wildfire, a trail of burned-out castles and broken promises. Nobility loved their drama. And when it all went wrong, they sent for commoners to clean up the mess. And Nyra had the feeling that's exactly why the king had sent his men to find her.

"I have," she replied, carefully. "What of him?"

Harmond and Jori exchanged glances, then looked around at the villagers who remained after the healing. They were clearly curious, ogling at the men in their fine clothes that the king had sent.

"Is there somewhere we can talk privately?" Harmond asked.

Nyra hesitated, then gave a short nod. "This way."

She led them across the square and down a narrow footpath edged with flowering thistles and low stone walls, her steps brisk despite the heat. The mayor followed at a respectful distance, dabbing his forehead with a handkerchief, while the two councilors walked in silence, their polished boots too fine for the dusty lane.

Her cottage stood at the edge of a grove, tucked among wind-bent birches and half-shadowed by a crooked elder tree. The small house was built of white-washed stone with a shingled roof patched in places with straw and thatching. They were humble, but solid little buildings. She pushed open the door and stepped inside, holding it for the others with a reluctant sweep of her arm.

"Mind the threshold," she muttered.

The interior was immaculately clean, though plainly furnished. The single room held a small hearth with a soot-darkened chimney, beside which sat a sturdy wooden table and two chairs worn smooth from use. A narrow shelf above the fireplace held a cluster of dried herbs bound in twine, a chipped teapot, and her grimoire. The kitchen area was barely more than a sideboard and a basin, with iron pots hanging neatly on pegs and a stack of folded cloths on the windowsill. No clutter, no ornamentation—only what was needed.

Nyra stood awkwardly for a beat as the men took in her home. She didn't say what she was thinking: that they probably slept in rooms larger than her entire house, with featherbeds and velvet drapes and silver spoons for stirring their tea. Here, everything had a purpose, and most things had more than one. There was no space for indulgence when coin went toward poultices and tinctures, not perfumes.

She gestured to the chairs. "Sit, please."

The councilors sat, Nyra and the mayor remained standing. Councilor Harmond wasted no time getting to the point. "Prince Rhezan suffers under a monstrous dragon curse. His entire form has been twisted by sorcery. You are invited—ordered, if you prefer a more accurate phrase—to travel to Varynth Hold and attempt to cure him of this affliction."

Nyra felt her heart jolt. A dragon curse? What the hell?

She had read about such transformations in ancient texts, but never had she encountered one firsthand. In fact, she wasn't sure she'd ever heard of one happening anywhere in the kingdom. She half-remembered references to grimoires locked away in private libraries that spoke of such things.

From the looks on the men's faces, they were not joking. The fact that they were entirely in earnest shocked and overwhelmed her. How in the name of the gods was she supposed to lift a dragon curse?

Nyra inhaled slowly, trying to remain calm. "You honor me by asking for my help, but I tend to many people here," she said, gesturing weakly out the window toward the village square. "They rely on my healing. There will be no one to help them if I leave."

The councilors stared at the mayor; they had obviously been told Nyra would agree with no hesitation. The mayor stuttered and stammered in reply. "We...uh...we can...we can call on the healer in the next village over." He gave Nyra a sharp look. "Best do what these men are asking you to do. We cannot say 'no' to His Majesty The King, now can we?"

Councilor Harmond frowned as he stared at Nyra. "See there? Problem solved. The entire kingdom's future depends on Prince Rhezan's recovery."

Jori cleared his throat in a more diplomatic tone. "We can pay you well. Ten thousand duckets. The king does not expect your help for free. He understands your livelihood depends on having resources for your patients."

At the mention of such a lavish sum, Nyra's breath

caught. Hope flared in her chest. She imagined the new medicines and expanded clinic she could set up with so much money. Yet the weight in her chest intensified. Was she truly prepared to walk away from her villages for a job she might not even be able to accomplish?

She folded her arms, determined to hold her ground. "I understand the prince's predicament, but I will not abandon my people. There are many here, and in surrounding villages, who are sick. And no matter what our esteemed mayor says," she glared at the man before continuing, "The next nearest healer is at least a three-day journey away. I am sorry. You'll have to find another healer to help you."

The privy councilors looked at each other and, with a heavy sigh, Harmond rose from his seat, crossed to the cottage door and opened it. He gestured at somebody outside and, a moment later, several armed soldiers with the king's sigil, a red dragon spitting fire, pinned to their doublets entered her home.

Harmond's expression hardened. He gestured discreetly to the soldiers, who edged closer. "Miss Nyra, you do not seem to grasp the gravity of this situation. Prince Rhezan's condition is not just a magical affliction. It is a crisis. The king commands you to come. He will accept no polite refusals."

The underlying threat caused the tiny hairs along Nyra's neck to stand on end. She saw the worry in the mayor's eyes. Her heartbeat thundered in her chest. Her entire life had been devoted to healing the sick, but she had never imagined being dragged into the king's demands to attempt to lift a curse she'd read about only in myths and legends. She cast a quick glance out the window at the crowd that was still gathered, watching her cottage to see what would happen next. The single ducket laying in her pouch weighed heavily on her conscience. How could she leave?

Looking back to Jori and Harmond, she tried once more to preserve her freedom. "I do not doubt your sincerity or the king's. Or the prince's suffering," she said, her voice wavering. "But I cannot simply abandon my duties here."

Councilor Jori's sigh was tinged with weary impatience. He was obviously not the sort of man who heard the word 'no' a lot. "If you continue to refuse, we have no choice but to enforce His Majesty's royal decree." He looked pointedly at the soldiers. "In which case, you will be clapped in irons and escorted, against your will, to Varynth Hold. Which would you prefer? Retaining a modicum of your freedom or losing it completely?"

The reality sent a cold jolt through Nyra's spine. She observed the soldiers' cautious but ready stances. Her gaze fell on the mayor, who hung his head and would not meet her eyes. He could do nothing to save her and still keep his own freedom.

Her mind raced. If they were ordered to take her by force, then the prince's curse was monstrous, indeed. Could she even cure something so immense? The texts she owned barely touched on curses of that scale. She thought she would never have to attempt them. And there was another piece of her magic—blood-magic—that she dared not mention. It was outlawed because it was volatile and dangerous in the wrong hands. She would not admit what she could do. Not to these councilors, nor to the townspeople she served.

It seemed there was only one choice if she wanted to protect herself and people she loved. She couldn't help anyone if she were thrown into prison. Nyra exhaled in defeat. "If there is no other way, I will go. Just...give me time to gather my things."

Councilor Harmond, with a guarded nod, gestured for the soldiers to stand at ease. Jori allowed a brief, triumphant smile to touch his lips. "We appreciate your cooperation. We leave at first light."

Before they left, Jori turned to Nyra and said, "We shall leave a contingent of soldiers here overnight. Just in case you...need assistance in packing your things."

Assistance. What a strange and threatening way to say 'don't even think about running.'

Nyra rose slowly. Her legs ached from kneeling so long in the relentless sun, and her heart felt heavier than stone in her chest. She tried to compose herself as the villagers watched with somber faces. Many could not fathom the idea of losing their only healer. Others stared at the king's soldiers with murmurs of worry.

She wished she could whisper comfort to every patient who currently needed her. The mayor cleared his throat and glanced at the councilors. He looked torn between an urge to protect Nyra and the fear of defying royal authority. "I'm sure if Nyra needs help to pack her belongings, there are neighbors who would be willing to help," he said quietly.

"Thank you, but no," she murmured. "I can manage."

After the privy councilors left her cottage, Nyra watched them go from the large window that faced out into the village square. Many of the villagers had already left, but a few of them stayed and appeared to be gawking at the armed guards outside her home.

Sweat beaded the back of Nyra's neck, and it wasn't from the heat. She felt her stomach flip and the urge to vomit overwhelmed her. She ran to her bedroom, and barely had time to grab the chamber pot from the corner before the contents of her stomach came up. When she had finished, she sat heavily on the edge of the mattress. She emptied the chamber pot, gave it a quick clean, then put the in the corner. Then, she curled up into a ball on her bed and cried her eyes out.

AN HOUR LATER, Nyra realized she needed to start packing. She knelt beside her bed and pulled a trunk her mother had left her and her satchel from beneath it. The weathered leather bag that had seen better days but held together where it counted. She packed her clothes into the trunk and then put the satchel on the table in the middle of the room and opened it. She ran her fingertips over the grimoire's faded runes on the front cover, feeling the tingle of magic that she had invoked countless times in smaller ways but never for something as daunting as a dragon curse. Blood-magic lingered in its pages too, a power she rarely dared to use. She prayed it would not come to that.

Then, put the grimoire into the bag, set vertically along the side of it so she could fit other things in, as needed, and still be able to pull the tome out during the journey to read if she wanted to.

Next, she reached for her shelf of jars and bundles, selecting only the most essential herbs. Moonpetal for infections. Poupur root, despite its stench, for fever and cramping. Valeric moss, sunberry, and a tightly tied pouch of dried frostvine. Into a small cloth roll she tucked a mortar and pestle wrapped in a linen square, along with a trio of vials filled with tinctures that shimmered faintly when turned to the light.

From beneath a floorboard, she retrieved a slim bundle wrapped in oilskin. Inside lay the things she never let anyone see—her grimoire that contained not only mundane spells, but the darker ones related to blood-magic, her ritual knife with its bone handle, her carved wooden runes, and a smooth stone worn flat from years of tracing sigils. These she tucked into a hidden compartment at the bottom of the satchel, pausing only to whisper a quiet charm over the flap before sealing it shut.

She laid a pair of extra shifts across the top, along with her mended wool cloak and the fingerless gloves she'd knitted herself during a long winter. Then she thought better of putting so many clothes into the satchel, and put the shifts into the trunk. She would wear the cloak if needed, or carry it with her. The gloves still went into the bag. Last, from the drawer beside her bed, she retrieved her locket. The tiny portrait inside had faded with time, but the soft curve of her mother's smile still showed through. Nyra pressed it to her lips before slipping it into a pocket of the satchel, near enough to touch when she needed courage.

Her pouch of coins followed. There wasn't much in it, twenty or so duckets. She didn't have much, and if she needed to run after she arrived at Varynth Hold she wasn't sure how far her coins would get her. Still, they were a fragment of independence she wasn't going to surrender.

She tried to steady her breathing. To be cursed into a dragon's form spoke volumes of the darkest of arts required to perform such a ritual. That thought, alone, filled her with dread. She wanted to run but the guards out front and out back—yes, she checked the back and they infested her garden like moles—would put her in chains if she tried. And who knew, she might not be the only one to suffer. If she defied the king, entire village might suffer retribution. She could not allow that.

The cottage felt hotter all of a sudden, but Nyra was sure it was the anxiety that had settled in her chest like a load of bricks. It wasn't hot outside, but inside it felt like a blacksmith's shop. Nyra steeled herself for the journey ahead. She would attempt the impossible: break a monstrous curse that imprisoned the king's son in a dragon's body. If she failed, the consequences would be devastating. And she could not shake the quiet truth inside her that to save Prince Rhezan, she might be forced to reveal a power she had always vowed to keep hidden.

TWO

Nyra stood at the door of her small cottage at first light, heart skittering like a restless sparrow's wings. Beyond the threshold, the day stretched out bright and merry with birds singing in the trees, as if they were trying to comfort her. Her satchel hung from her shoulder. Though she had answered countless urgent knocks over the ten years she had been the village healer. She was young by her own measurement, only five-and-twenty years old, and though she'd earned her patients' trust through skill and consistency, she knew she was still considered a spinster which was almost worse than having Fogrot. She thought of the countless coughing children, accident victims, and elders on the brink of death, and she knew nothing she had ever done prepared her for what she would face with the dragon prince's curse.

She glanced around her tidy front room one final time. A few wooden shelves displayed rows of carefully labeled herbs. A small table, where she mixed salves for local ailments, sat empty. Nearby, the last medicinal notes she'd written lay pinned under a half-spent candle. She'd almost forgotten to pack them. She grabbed them quickly and stuffed them into her bag. With one last sweep of her gaze, she stepped forward, letting the door click shut behind her.

Outside, the two privy councilors in their fine cloaks waited with a squad of soldiers. Councilor Jori looked tense, like he'd expected her to bolt, but then a big smile of relief spread ear-to-ear when he saw her. "Miss Nyra." He bowed at the waist, then straighted up. "Time is precious, and the king awaits your presence in Varynth Hold."

Nyra clutched the strap of her satchel. "I am ready," she said softly, though her heart felt anything but. She inhaled, summoning a composure she did not fully feel. Years of being a healer had prepared her for any situation, but nothing had prepared her for the possibility of leaving the village, and traveling into the forbidding Drakareth Mountains under a royal summons she couldn't ignore.

Councilor Harmond saw her trunk sitting just inside the door of her cottage then snapped at two soldiers who immediately picked it up and carried it to the carriage, where they secured it to the boot with heavy ropes. The sight of the carriage nearly stole her breath away. It was a stately coach drawn by four white horses. Gilded trim around the windows sparkled in the morning light, and the crimson dragon crest of King Vorian's court, emblazoned on the carriage door, was also highlighted with gilt. Never had Nyra imagined traveling in such luxury.

"The horses are restless this morning," Harmond said. "We should get on our way."

She paused to take a steadying breath, then accepted a soldier's hand as she climbed inside, settling her satchel beneath the cushioned bench where she sat. Harmond and Jori climbed inside the carriage and sat opposite her. When they were ready, and the soldiers had mounted their horses, Alistar reached through an open window and rapped smartly on the side of the carriage. The horses lurched into motion with a jolt that rocked the cabin, their hooves striking the packed earth in a steady, rhythmic clatter as the carriage began its slow roll out of the village.

The interior startled her with its elegance. Plush seats of deep burgundy velvet lined the walls, and ornamental tassels framed the small, curtained windows. Subtle patterns in golden thread traced dragons curled around vines, an image that made her stomach clench at the memory of why she was traveling. The extravagance both fascinated her and filled her with a nagging anxiety. If a mere carriage reflected this level of wealth, what would the royal fortress be like?

The carriage creaked as it rolled past the stone well and continued along the well-worn path leading out of the village. Villagers had gathered quietly along the path. Word of Nyra's departure and the reason for it had obviously spread quickly. Some bowed their heads, others raised a hand in solemn farewell. A few children waved, their expressions a mix of confusion and sadness. Nyra met their eyes only briefly, her throat tightening as she gripped the edge of her seat.

Children chased the coach and waved, shouting their goodbyes. Nyra forced herself to memorize each face as she looked through the back window. Her heart grew heavier. Would they find another healer? Would the next crisis, an accident or a wave of the dreaded pox, overwhelm them without her care? The children stopped following when the carriage crossed the village border, and Nyra waved at them until the it rounded the next bend.

She turned to face the privy councilors once more and bit her lip to keep from crying. Harmond and Jori were busy looking anywhere but at her, and Nyra swore silently that she would return to her village as soon as she could, if the gods and their fates allowed. The carriage turned onto the northern road. Soon, she could see only the dust kicked up by the horses' hooves when she looked out the back window.

The air already felt felt too warm inside the carriage. Harmond busied himself with reading a stack of letters. Jori arranged his cloak neatly around his shoulders, then glanced at her.

"We understand this is difficult for you," he offered after several moments. "But your assistance is invaluable."

Nyra twisted her fingers in her lap, uncertain how to respond. Instead of voicing the torrent of worry swirling in her mind, she gave him a small nod. The councilors exchanged a quick look, then turned their attention to the documents they carried. It seemed they had no desire to chat with her at all. It looked to be a long, lonely journey.

For the first few hours, the carriage rattled along,

carrying them across familiar plains that slowly gave way to rolling hills. Nyra kept the curtains drawn aside, quietly watching farmland pass by. The farms gradually gave way to pockets of forest, where tall birches and twisted oaks lined the road, their leaves whispering in the breeze. Nyra usually found peace in these woods—the hush between trees, the filtered sunlight, the earthy scent of moss and bark. But today, there wasn't a shred of calm to be found. Every branch seemed to loom, every shadow pressed too close.

When the morning sun rose a little higher, and it was easier to read in the carriage, Nyra tentatively opened her satchel and pulled out her grimoire. The worn leather cover felt comforting under her fingertips. She had collected so many notes on healing, standard spells, and even the barest references to curses that blended mortal blood with draconic magic. Her anxiety eased a fraction whenever she immersed herself in the text. She spent much of the first day's travel reading, turning page after page in search of any clue that might prepare her for the dragon affliction awaiting her at Varynth Hold.

Time soon blurred. They stopped for the night at a roadside inn, a small place that smelled of beer and wild garlic. It was staffed by a tired-eyed woman and her three sons. Harmond and Jori insisted Nyra take the room with the best bed, aware that a long journey would leave her exhausted before they even reached the fortress if she didn't get a good night's rest. Nyra lay awake for hours, though, her mind spiralling with questions about the prince, about dragon curses, and about how she would gather the strength to face it.

The next day they reached a town, and stayed at a lively coach inn used by merchants traveling north. The pattern continued: ride throughout the day, pause at inns along winding roads, and press onward again the next day. The Drakareth Mountains began appearing in the distance as looming, snow-capped shapes. Nyra watched them with equal parts dread and awe. The closer they got to the mountains, the more she mourned leaving her old life behind.

During one midday lull, the carriage bumped along a rough portion of road, and Nyra found herself staring at the page of her text without truly reading. Impulsively, she glanced across at the councilors, both scribbling notes. "Sorry to bother you," she said. "May I... ask something about Prince Rhezan?"

Jori looked up. Harmond paused too, waiting for the question.

Nyra twisted a fold of her skirt between her fingers. "I know the curse upon the prince is serious. But how did it happen? Who would cast such an evil thing on him, and why?"

The councilors exchanged a wary glance. Jori cleared his throat. "We do know who cast it," he said. "A witch from a distant province who once lived in our land cursed our prince. Her name was Selivera, and she was skilled in dark magic. For a while, she and the prince were entangled in... a brief affair."

Harmond picked up the thread. His tone was clipped,

suggesting he really didn't want to discuss the matter. "The king forbade the match because Selivera did not have noble blood. The woman did not take kindly to being rejected. In her rage, she cursed Prince Rhezan."

"Transformed him," Jori corrected. "It was no small hex. From what we understand, the magic was intricate, far beyond a typical shapeshifting spell. Since that day, the prince has been trapped in a dragon's body, but he retains his own mind and power of speech. He can shift sizes to some degree, but he has never escaped his dragon form."

Nyra swallowed. She remembered the fleeting references in her texts to curses that fused mortals with powerful creatures. She had never pictured it so vividly, nor that it could be inflicted with such passionate scorn. "For how long has he lived with this curse?" she asked. Her throat felt too dry.

"Fifteen years that have felt like fifteen hundred," Jori replied.

Harmond stared at his folded hands. "Too long," he said softly.

"Has anyone tried to lift the curse?" she asked. "I mean, the king must have employed other mages or healers over the years."

"He has," Harmond said, flatly. "They all failed."

A somber hush settled in the carriage. Nyra's mind swam with questions she dared not speak because both men had returned to their letters, a sign they were done discussing the matter. Could she undo magic so potent it had resisted every attempt to undo it so far? She struggled to keep her expression calm, unwilling to show the councilors the mix of fascination and fear churning inside her. Even so, she felt the watchful weight of their stares as they occasionally glanced at her. They must have guessed she was uneasy, but she refused to let them see her panic.

That evening, the coach rumbled into Carcassonne, a medieval town set in the foothills of the mountains. A slow sunset painted the high walls and narrow cobbled streets in gold and pink hues. The King's Arms Coach Inn awaited them just inside the gate. A stable groom hurried to tend to the horses as Nyra, the last out of the carriage, gazed around at clusters of townsfolk finishing their day's business. She noticed vendors closing sturdy wooden shutters, a trio of travellers bartering for supplies, and the faint aroma of spiced apples drifting from a booth near the gate.

The inn itself bustled with activity. Wooden beams crisscrossed the large common room, and the hum of conversation rumbled below the steady crackling of a blazing hearth. Tired from the journey, Nyra set her satchel at her feet and stretched the ache from her shoulders. Jori arranged for rooms. Once settled in her room, Nyra ventured downstairs again to the inn's main hall rather than isolating herself in her cramped quarters. She found the privy councilors at a corner table and joined them, her stomach growling, enticed by the scent of roasted meat and fresh bread.

Nyra took the offered cup from the innkeeper with both hands. She sniffed its contents cautiously—sweet, but sharp—and took a tentative sip. The flavor bloomed across her tongue: honey-rich with a lingering burn that crept in like a whisper of smoke. She blinked in surprise, then took another, fuller mouthful.

"This is…" She paused, searching for the word. "Gods, what is this? It's like spiced fire."

Councilor Harmond gave a rare smile. "Ginger mead. Imported from the southern coast. The monks at Redwall Abbey brew it—when they're not setting themselves on fire trying to improve the recipe."

"It's medicine," Jori added dryly, raising his own cup. "Or so they claim. Fortifies the blood and wards off colds. And common sense, too, if you drink too much of it."

Nyra took another sip anyway. Her lips tingled, and for the first time since she left home, the tight knot in her chest began to loosen.

As she ate, Nyra cast cautious glances at the councilors. Something in her yearned to know more about the prince, more than just the results of a tragic love affair. "Did prince ever have… a kinder nature? Before he was a dragon," she ventured quietly, sipping her cider.

Jori nodded. "Yes. Prince Rhezan was a figure of grace at court. Intelligent, a patron of the arts, well-liked by everyone." He paused, voice lowering. "He was a soldier, once. He fought in small skirmishes, defending our border villages. Many admired him for his willingness to stand with ordinary soldiers."

"It is all the more heartbreaking to see him now," Harmond added between bites of stew. "That bright spirit buried beneath his fury."

Nyra listened in silence, her food growing cold. Her medical knowledge told her that curses often warped not only the body but also the mind. How much of Rhezan's wounded soul was truly from the effects of monstrous magic, and how much was from despair? They were probably linked, the mind, heart, and body were always linked. Hers was the daunting task of trying to unravel the magic without causing the prince even more harm. The burden weighed on her thoughts, pressing on her heart like a lead weight.

FOR THE REMAINDER of their journey, she dug deeper into her grimoire and the other ancient texts she'd brought with her. She scribbled marginal notes, cross-referenced sketches of draconic glyphs, and tried to glean any hint of how best to treat a man partially trapped in a dragon's form. The days grew cooler, the skies more overcast, and the roads steadily climbed into rocky terrain.

Two weeks after they'd left Redwick, they passed through a narrow pass where the wind shrieked, and at last a colossal fortress came into view. Varynth Hold was built into the mountainside, and stood like a watchful sentinel over a valley below. Its ancient walls climbed high and disappeared into the dark rock above, with scattered towers bristling from the cliff's face. Nyra caught her breath. It was impossible to guess how many rooms hid behind those mighty gates.

The carriage stopped and the imposing gates creaked open. Beyond the gates, guards in crimson and gold livery hurried to clear the path as the carriage rolled forward, slowing only when it reached the inner entrance of the castle fortress, which loomed over a vast stone courtyard. Jori and Harmond stepped out of the carriage. Nyra followed, blinking as she took in the fortress's size. Thick curtains of ivy draped over sections of the stone, but otherwise the place looked stark. She wondered which windows concealed watchers peering down at her arrival.

Two stewards approached, nodding politely as they hefted Nyra's luggage from the boot and carried it into the castle. Nyra refused the offer to also take her satchel, preferring to keep it close to her. The councilors turned to her. Jori stood with hands folded behind his back.

"You have had a long journey," he said. "Follow the stewards. They will escort you to your room. The beds in Varynth Hold are the finest anywhere. You should be able to sleep well tonight."

"Better than in the coach inns, that's for sure," Harmond added. "In the morning, you will meet Prince Rhezan. Good evening, Miss Nyra."

She managed a small bow of gratitude before the privy councilors left her with the stewards. "Thank you." Her throat tightened. The prospect of finally meeting the cursed prince set her pulse thumping with a mix of dread and curiosity.

The stewards led her into a vaulted entry hall floored with polished stone. Torches flickered, casting shifting shadows on the walls, revealing glimpses of carved arches and high ceilings. The cold in the enormous drafty hall felt more intense than any place she had known. Nyra's was breathless with the furnishings in every room. Tapestries woven in threads of gold hung every few steps, depicting old kings crowned with ornate helms, or stylized dragons interwoven with swirling runes. She was too overwhelmed to take it all in at once.

Then, echoing from somewhere deep within the fortress, came a terrible sound—a roar that raked through her mind, equal parts agony and fury. Nyra froze, heart leaping. The cry reverberated off the stone, turning into a wailing howl that prickled at every hair on her arms.

"What was that?" she gasped, turning to one of the stewards.

He paled visibly, swallowing. "That would be Prince Rhezan, mistress. He is not in the best mood tonight."

The other steward's nervous laugh did little to ease her shivers. "He tends to vent his temper after sundown," he offered. "We have grown used to it. I hope it won't disturb your sleep."

Nyra's head spun at the thought that the roar belonged not to any caged beast, but to the man she had come to heal. She forced her feet to move again, albeit shakily. The stewards continued up a wide stone staircase, then along a hallway adorned with gilded mirrors. They paused at a door of dark polished wood, pushing it open to reveal a spacious chamber. Candlelit sconces revealed a grand canopied bed draped in deep crimson linens and a table holding a simple meal of bread and cheese. The sumptuous rug beneath her feet made her feel out of place, as if she might soil it simply by standing there. She noticed her trunk had been placed at the foot of her bed.

The stewards bowed and one of them said, "If you

need anything, ring the bell by the door. Servants will come to tend to your needs."

"We have seamstresses and a laundry here at Varynth Hold, if you need them," the other said. "You will also find court-appropriate clothes in there." He pointed at the tallest wardrobe Nyra had ever seen.

Nyra nodded absently, trying to take it all in. "Thank you."

Once they were gone, she crossed the room in a daze. The bed looked luxurious, far finer than the stiff bed she had in her cottage. She eyed the large wardrobe carved with serpentine dragons. Inside, she found dresses and cloaks in fine fabrics: velvet, brocade, and soft linens in shades of forest green, midnight blue, and deep gold. It seemed the king had spared no effort to prepare her accommodations. Still, she felt uneasy about wearing garments so obviously tailored for a noblewoman, which she was not.

Her empty stomach growled, so she turned to the table and nibbled on the cheese and bread, washing them down with cool water. With each bite, she thought of the villagers at home, who often went hungry on rough nights. The clash between her past world and her new circumstances left a bitter taste in her mouth.

Aware that dawn would bring more challenges, she tugged off her cloak and moved to the washbasin. The water was cold but refreshing as she scrubbed the dust of travel from her body with a cloth. Every motion reminded her that she was no longer living simply. Every breath teased her with the faint smell of old stone and the haunting echo of that terrible roar.

Finally, she dressed for bed, slipping into a linen shift that felt crisp against her skin. She blew out several candles, leaving only a faint glow near the bedside. Easing under the thick covers, she sank into the goose-down mattress with a shock of comfort. But her mind, restless with worry, refused to let her relax. Prince Rhezan was somewhere in this fortress, thoroughly miserable if the night's roar was any indication.

She laid a hand against her chest, focusing on her empathic senses. There, in the quiet pulse of the night, she detected a faint ripple of rage radiating through the fortress stone. The seething undercurrent made her heart pound. She had felt others' pain before, but never something this potent. Each ragged surge from the depths told of conflict coiled within the prince, a torment that left him keening into the dark.

A fresh roar tore through the walls, louder this time, echoing with unbridled anguish. Nyra pressed her eyes shut. Fear coiled in her stomach. She had accepted the call to heal him, but what if her magic wasn't enough? She pictured his cursed state in her mind, and wondered about the dark magic that had led to his monstrous transformation. Dread told her she might be stepping into a labyrinth of powerplays and pain she had only glimpsed so far.

The echoes faded, and the fortress settled into uneasy stillness. She tried to slow her breathing and recall the comforting hush of her village, yet she could not dispel the image of scaled wings and burning eyes, or the knowledge that this place would test her skills and her courage to their limits. Without answers, with only her battered grimoire and resolve, she drifted into a shallow, fitful sleep.

In the last moment of awareness, she silently asked herself: What have I gotten myself into? And as if in response, the memory of that roar rumbled through her thoughts, a reminder that when morning came, she would face the prince behind that anguished cry whether she was ready or not.

THREE

Nyra woke to the soft chime of metal on stone in the hallway outside her chamber. At first, she did not move from the bed. Finally, she forced herself upright, noticing the tray of breakfast on a small table near the window. Someone had brought fresh bread, a small bowl of pottage thick with meat and vegetables, and a cup of faintly steaming tea.

She bowed her head, releasing a shaky exhale. Someone had been in her room and it hadn't woke her. She must have been more exhausted than she thought. Nyra ate quickly, although the taste of bread was as bland as ash on her tongue. Outside her window, morning light barely broke through the thick mountain mists. She had never seen a fortress perched so high that the clouds settled right below her window. It felt unnatural, as though Varynth Hold stood halfway between two worlds.

Finishing her tea, Nyra gathered her courage. She pulled on a the royal blue dress and donned a pair of blue silk slippers. She tried to open the door but it was locked. Where they thought she might escape to from this seemingly impenetrable fortress, given the forbidding mountain passes they traversed on the journey, she had no idea. She would have to wait for whatever summons came.

It wasn't long before there were several sharp knocks on the door. A moment later, Harmond entered. He hadn't even waited for her to say 'come in.' Harmond was dressed in a deep-green cloak draped, and his face was so serious, Nyra didn't dare smile at him. He nodded briskly, looking impatient.

"Miss Nyra, I've come to escort you to meet Prince Rhezan," he said. "Please, come with me."

"Shouldn't I meet the king, first? He may wish to talk about Prince Rhezan's...um...condition. You know, before I meet him."

Harmond chuckled, then gestured for her to follow, which she did. "King Vorian thinks it would be better for you to meet his son first. Come along, we have no time to dilly dally."

Though her pulse throbbed in her throat, Nyra did not argue further. She followed him into the corridor. Two guards trailed behind them, their boots echoing ominously against the stone floor. They descended several winding flights of stairs, the walls were illuminated by torches that sputtered and she was so anxious she nearly choked on her spit when she swallowed. Each turn down the stairs brought a new draft of damp chill, as if the fortress breathed ice from every corridor.

The castle wasn't quiet. It wasn't just the servants and

courtiers going from this place to that that made it noisy. The entire fortress seemed to hum with the tinnitus of underlying magic, a subtle vibration that crawled up Nyra's spine and made her edgy. She tried to steady her breathing. The drum of her heart seemed deafening, but she kept her eyes open, observing every detail of the descent into the lower caverns of the castle.

The passage narrowed, its architecture shifting into older stone framed with veins of black obsidian. Flickers of torchlight glimmered in those veins, giving the illusion of trapped embers. She could not shake the impression that the rock itself pulsed with a dark presence, an old power laced through the fortress walls. With each step, Nyra felt a deeper bite of cold that was not merely the mountain climate. Something more ancient and menacing lurked here.

They passed under a low arch leading into an even darker tunnel. Harmond spared her a quick look over his shoulder. "Stay close. These passages can wind for miles." His voice vibrated with caution. "It is in the deeper halls in the mountain that Prince Rhezan finds most comfort."

Nyra swallowed. "Comfort?" She could not imagine any mortal, cursed or otherwise, feeling at ease in such a dreary place. The walls pressed inward, the scant torch-light barely holding back the gloom.

Harmond answered in a quiet tone, "He is used to the darkness in the deep caverns. Few from the castle venture down here. Only the king, Jori, me, and a few guards." He paused a moment. "And now you."

Another guard waited at a T-shaped intersection of

corridors, holding a torch. He nodded respectfully to Harmond. The guard gestured for them to follow, then turned left at an intersection of four passageways. The air grew heavier until Nyra's breathing strained. She could almost hear magic's heartbeat in her ears, which was a curious thing. She didn't often encounter buildings that were embedded with magic that had been cast within their walls. The last time she did was at her mother's funeral.

It had started with a knock at their cottage door—urgent, trembling. The Halloway family, across town, had all taken ill, one after another, with a fever that no herb or charm could break. Eight of them, packed under one roof: parents, grandparents, children. Inetra had packed her satchel before Nyra could finish asking what herbs she'd need. "You stay here," she had said, kissing Nyra's forehead. "I'll be back in a few days."

She didn't return in a few days. She returned nearly two weeks later, gaunt and glass-eyed, shoulders hunched with exhaustion, hands shaking. Only the youngest of the Halloway children, a boy of twelve, had survived. "He'll need care," Inetra had whispered as she crossed the threshold. "But I need to sleep first. Just a little sleep."

By morning, she was burning with fever. Nyra had tried everything. Steeped teas of elderberry and willow bark, wiped her mother's brow with cool water, rubbed her hands and feet to coax the chill away. She used every remedy her mother had ever taught her. But Inetra had poured too much of herself into saving others, and there was nothing left for Nyra to save.

On the third night, Inetra woke briefly. Her eyes found Nyra's in the half-dark. "Do not be afraid, my little dove. You already know how to be a healer," she murmured. "You always did." Then she closed her eyes and didn't open them again.

Nyra stayed by her side until the breath truly stopped, until her tears dried into silence, until the cottage smelled only of herbs and death. She buried her mother's heart in the old grove the next morning, weeping into the loamy soil as dawn broke.

The funeral was held in the clearing just beyond the edge of the village, where the cedar trees leaned in as if to listen and the earth was soft with old moss and memory. Nyra stood barefoot on the frostbitten grass, fifteen and barely holding herself upright, her mother's shawl wrapped tight around her shoulders. It still smelled faintly of rose hips and juniper, of long nights hunched over boiling kettles and herb bundles, of comfort. Of home.

They had laid Inetra out on a bier of cedar branches, wrapped in the ceremonial linen, her gentle hands folded over her chest with a sprig of lavender tucked between her fingers. Her skin was waxen, pale but peaceful, and it was more peace than Nyra had seen on her mother's face in months.

The villagers came in small, quiet groups, heads bowed, offerings clutched awkwardly in hand. Some left herbs. A few left coins. Most left nothing because they had nothing to give, they simply murmured soft words of thanks. Inetra had been healer to them all. She had stitched their wounds, eased their coughs, grieved with them over their stillborns, and whoever could pay coin, did. Those who bartered in livestock or favors.

The priest had offered to speak, but Nyra gently declined. It wasn't out of resentment—she liked him well enough, and he had always spoken kindly of her mother. But this farewell was hers to give. She needed to find the words herself, even if they came out rough and raw.

"She was kind," Nyra had said, stumbling through the simple speech. "She was brave. And she tried to heal everyone, no matter the risk to her."

That was all. She couldn't say more. Her throat had closed around the words she couldn't give shape to—the loneliness already taking root in her ribs, the guilt that would not stop gnawing. After the funeral pyre was lit and the scent of burning cedar rose into the sky, Nyra sat by the her mother's ashes until the stars came out, her fingers tracing patterns in the soot, waiting for a voice that would never come again.

No one had let her grieve alone. The village had gathered for the funeral, and in the days that followed, many came bearing offers—extra food, spare blankets, even a room in their homes. A few had gently urged her to leave the cottage, saying it might be too full of ghosts for someone so young. But Nyra couldn't leave. The worn floorboards, the herb-stained table, the fire that still smelled like her mother's teas—they were all she had left. She stayed.

She was fifteen, and though her neighbors tried to soften the edges of her loss, she had been on her own ever since.

AFTER WHAT FELT like an eternity of walking through twisting passageways, they arrived at the mouth of an enormous cavern. Faint runes were etched into a stone arch that marked the boundary of the cavern, and Nyra craned her neck to get a better look at them.

"There will be time enough later for you to decipher the runes. Prince Rhezan is waiting," Harmond reminded her.

Nyra followed him, overwhelmed by the immensity of the space. There was an enormous mangled iron gate hanging off its hinges on both sides of the entrance. It looked like something gigantic and angry had fought its way through it, and Nyra figured that something was Rhezan.

Torches mounted on jagged outcroppings revealed walls marked with unfamiliar symbols. Obsidian shards jutted from the stone in shapes reminiscent of claws. Flickers of something like firelight gleamed in the distance, reflecting on dark pools where water had collected over the years. A quiet deeper than Nyra had ever known blanketed the chamber, like the eerie silence before a storm.

Harmond stopped, and gestured for her to do the same. "We wait here until Prince Rhezan makes himself known." His gaze flicked around warily. "Mind your distance, Miss Nyra. He can spit fire farther than you think."

She did not have to wonder what he meant. A sudden flare of crimson heat lit one wall, followed by a deafening roar that vibrated through her ribcage. Nyra's eyes widened. A colossal shape emerged from the shadows: an immense dragon coiled across the far side of the cavern with scales like polished obsidian. The edges of his scales glowed faintly, as if rimmed with molten metal. His golden eyes snapped open, and they burned with more fury than any living creature she had seen. Flame licked at the corners of his jaws.

Harmond and the guards retreated behind a rock formation, presumably in search of cover. Nyra's legs threatened to fold beneath her. No one had adequately prepared her for the sheer size and power of Rhezan in his dragon state. His roar rolled through the cavern like thunder, shaking loose tiny fragments of stone from the ceiling.

She forced herself to take one step forward, ignoring the councilor's hiss of warning. Her heart hammered so forcefully that her vision blurred, but she managed a trembling introduction that echoed off the cavern walls, addressing him by name. "Prince Rhezan," she called, her voice unsteady. "I am Nyra, your father hired me to help you." Her words sounded small in the vastness of the chamber.

The dragon's eyes narrowed, and he snarled, unleashing a wave of flames that splashed across the far wall. The intense heat washed over Nyra's face, making her wince. The force of it rattled every nerve in her body. She glimpsed the raw power coiled within him. If he chose to, he could reduce her to ash with a single gust of that flaming breath.

He spoke in a deep, rumbling tone that reverberated inside her chest. "Help from outside Varynth Hold? Another false salvation?"

Nyra wet her lips, struggling to sound calm. "I... am a healer. The best I can do is try. If you will let me, I want to try lifting your curse." She had expected him to be hostile, but something about hearing the pain in his voice struck her harder than she anticipated.

Rhezan's scaled tail lashed across the stone, flinging sparks as it scraped. "Your kind has paraded through here in years past. They babble about potions and incantations. They fail." His glowing eyes pinned her in place. "And so will you."

Her hands trembled at her sides. "I—I may not live up to your expectations, but I promise I will do everything in my power," she managed. She loathed how weak her voice sounded, quivering with anxiety. "Please, if you—"

A snarl cut her off, followed by a tremor rolling through the floor. She barely held her balance. "Do not beg me for anything," he snarled. "I did not summon you. My father did." The mention of King Vorian sent a fresh flick of flame curling from his nostrils. "He clutches at any last hope of saving me, not caring how many times I endure false cures. If you value your life, do not meddle in mine."

His words stung with fierce bitterness. She opened her mouth to answer, but fear swallowed her voice. She felt so small, so inadequate. Harmond signaled frantically to her, urging her to stand back. But Nyra wanted to reason with Rhezan, to show him she was not an opportunistic pretender. She wanted to say she understood that hope could feel like a cruel trick when repeated failures overshadowed it. But his eyes burned too fiercely and it made her feel faint.

In the end, the only sound that escaped her was a soft, helpless breath. Rhezan's rumbling growl echoed through the caverns. He uncoiled, rising to a scale-ridged height that dwarfed everything around them, then struck the ground with both forelimbs. Red sparks flared near his claws. Darkness roiled around him like a living aura. That display of wrath was not aimed at her directly, but it might as well have been a barrier shutting her out.

Nyra's frayed nerves finally surrendered. She backpedaled, stumbling in her haste. The guards hovered anxiously behind the rock formation, their expressions grim. She rushed toward them, heart slamming. One of the guards shouted, then ushered her toward the stone arch leading to safety. Her courage collapsed into a twisting dread in her stomach.

"How can I heal someone who refuses help?" she murmured. No one answered. Within the cavern, Rhezan's furious roars continued, laced with sparks of flame that spiraled across the walls.

They walked back into the torchlit tunnel. Harmond's stoic demeanor wavered only a moment. "Come, Miss Nyra," he said curtly, turning to climb the path they had taken. "You have met the prince. Now you must decide how to work with him."

Nyra pressed a hand to her feverish forehead. "I cannot do this. I cannot." Her voice cracked with desperation. "Take me back to my village. My patients need me. I do not belong here."

The man's lips thinned, giving no room for sympathy. "You are not free to leave until the curse is lifted. That is the king's decision." He glanced at the two guards, who took immediate steps closer to her.

Nyra's pulse spiked with anger, fear, and frustration. "Don't make me a prisoner," she pleaded, though she heard her own voice faltering.

"We will care for you, keep you safe as much as possible," Harmond replied, calmly, "but you are not free to go."

She could think of no words strong enough to show her rage. She wanted to shout that the prince was unstoppable, that no healer could lift a curse that had been left to fester for so long. Instead, her limbs felt numb as the guards closed in on either side, guiding her away from from the cave. Her protest died in her throat.

The trek up the winding corridors blurred past in a haze of torches and flickering shadows. Each step felt heavier. She found herself replaying the image of Rhezan's red-tipped black scales and molten eyes, hearing the scorn in his voice as he dismissed her. The walls seemed to close around her, as though the fortress itself was alive with watchful malice. She could not breathe without tasting echoes of dust and old magic in the air.

At last, they reached the more familiar hallways near

her chamber. The guards opened her door, gestured politely for her to enter, then closed the door and locked her in. Nyra paced her gilded cage, feeling more trapped than ever. Her entire world had shrunk to these opulent walls—silken drapes, plush carpets, thick tapestries—and the knowledge that the dragon prince, in all his raw fury, waited in the caverns below. She remembered the heat of his flames, the finality in his words when he commanded her to leave.

Her frustration boiled over. "I need to get out of here," she whispered, envisioning the farmland of her village, the people who relied on her. Then she saw a memory of that monstrous tail lashing, and the cascade of fire he breathed. If she ran, would her people suffer for her refusal to obey the king? She pressed a trembling hand to her lips, blinking back tears. She felt powerless and alone.

Nyra's gaze fell on her battered grimoire resting on the bedside table. If she failed, would the king blame her for any misfortune that befell the realm? Would Rhezan do worse? She snatched the book up, trying to focus on simpler healing charms. She flipped through pages, scanning incantations as if she might find an immediate solution to a curse that had resisted the efforts of so many others. Her eyes scanned over the familiar recipes for potions and tinctures and then the rituals that were more powerful than any single magical intervention. Nothing in those pages spelled out how to soothe a man who had become part dragon, least of all how to thaw his white-hot resentment over his predicament.

Her frustration mounted until reading became impossible. She tossed the grimoire onto the bed and paced again. Her mind whirled with thoughts of picking the door lock and sneaking past the guards, but none of it was realistic. Even if she slipped away, she would never make it through the fortress gates alone. And if she somehow managed that, she would not make it through the mountains. They would kill her. Then there was the king's retribution on her village which would surely befall them if she somehow managed to get home. She forced her trembling to subside with slow, measured breaths.

Eventually, exhaustion replaced her anger. She sat on the bed, letting her hands graze the embossed cover of the grimoire once more. A strange vibration tingled beneath her fingertips. At first, she thought it was her racing pulse. Then she realized the sensation pulsed up through the floor and vibrated the bed. She rose, curiosity warring with dread, and placed her palm against the wooden paneling.

The moment she touched it, a faint wave of wrong energy surged along her arm. She yanked her fingers back, heart hammering. The magical signature thrumming in the walls was not hers. It was something else. Something ancient and malevolent. It prickled at her senses in a way that made her skin crawl.

She pressed her hand lightly on the wall to confirm, and again sensed churning pulses of darkness. Something lay buried deep in the stones beneath the finery on the walls. It was no gentle wellspring of power. This was something twisted, a residue of ancient rituals or old curses that never left. She could almost sense it breathing.

Nyra stepped back from the wall and a shiver raced down her spine. She realized how naive she was to think the castle fortress only contained the wrathful presence of an embittered prince. The walls themselves seemed to hide a deeper corruption. Fear pressed into her chest. It had grown darker outside, and a thunderous rain began to fall. She lit a candle by the bedside using a sulphur-tipped splint in the drawer of the bedside table. She washed her face, hoping the cool water would chase away her clammy anxiety. Instead, her features reflected in the basin's water looked drenched in worry.

She changed into a plain linen shift and doused the candle on the bedside table. The bed covers felt far too luxurious for someone who wished only to be back on the humble cot in her cottage. She lay on her side, gaze unfocused, tears blurring the shapes of the velvet canopy overhead.

Nothing had prepared her for this place. She had come under threat, yes, but part of her had believed she might at least do good. Now, the weight of her predicament sank in fully: Rhezan, consumed by rage and distrust; the king's cold desperation; and the living darkness that seemed to stir in these walls.

Tears slid down her cheeks, hot with despair. She tried to swallow them back, but her emotions would not be contained. It felt as though the fortress pulsed with a cruel heartbeat, reminding her of its power and her helplessness. She buried her face in the pillows, feeling each breath quake through her. She let silent sobs shake her unguarded, if only for a minute.

In the distance, she thought she heard another roar, muffled by innumerable tons of rock. Perhaps that was her imagination, or maybe the dragon prince really was unleashing more fury on the empty cavern. Either way, the sound tightened the knot in her chest. She realized, as she blinked away fresh tears, that she did not merely fear Rhezan's fire or the king's commands. If the magic in this place was truly alive, she dreaded the possibility that every stone in Varynth Hold might work against her, a silent legion of old magic waiting to strangle her best efforts to heal the prince.

She closed her eyes, letting exhaustion drag her deeper into restless submission. The last coherent thought that flickered across her mind was that the mountain had chosen to entomb Rhezan's misery, and she was the lone outsider forced to dig him out of it. The silence of her lovely bedchamber offered no consolation.

With tears still damp on her cheeks, Nyra finally surrendered to her tangled emotions, drifting into an uneasy half-sleep. Far below, another roar rose through the stone, as if the fortress itself cried in mourning. Her heart clenched, knowing she was already far beyond any comfort she had ever known. The monstrous power of the cursed prince, the stifling demands of the king, and the hidden darkness within Varynth Hold had sealed her fate.

CHAPTER

FOUR

Nyra closed her eyes, willing her body to surrender to sleep, but the restless ache in her muscles refused to let her drift away. The luxurious bed was too soft, the linens too fine, and she longed for home. Her thoughts circled around the events of the day before, colliding with the memory of the angry dragon prince and the echoes of Harmond's threats. Again and again, the fortress's simmering magic pressed against her senses, surging beneath the stone floors as though the walls themselves had a pulse.

Eventually, she gave up trying to go back to sleep. She swung her legs over the edge of the bed, letting her feet find the cool floor. The thick silence of the chamber amplified the sound of her sigh. Moonlight fell through the tall window, illuminating the bed's crimson drapes. She didn't know exactly how long she'd been locked in her room, but it couldn't have been long because her eyes felt gritty in the way they did when she hadn't had enough sleep. Anxiety had woken h er in the middle of the night, her heart still pounded with adrenaline, and she could not bear another hour of tense idleness looking at the walls.

Nyra put a dressing gown from the wardrobe over her shift and shuffled into a pair of satin slippers. Then she padded across the room, determined not to waste the night tossing in anguish. If she could not sleep, she might at least find more information about the curse. Perhaps the castle's library would hold a better clue than her own notes and magical texts.

Her hand closed around the door latch and she pulled. As expected, it did not budge. She muttered a few choice words under her breath. It was insulting enough that King Vorian and his councilors insisted she accept this "invitation" to the mountains. The locked door put a final exclamation point on how little freedom she could expect while being their prisoner guest.

She gave the door a few solid knocks, then stood back to see if a guard might answer or ignore her. At first, there was nothing. She rapped again. Moments later, a dull thump sounded, followed by a muffled voice.

"All right, all right," someone grumbled on the other side. "I hear you."

A key scraped in the lock. The door cracked open, revealing a broad-shouldered guard holding a torch. He peered at her with wary curiosity. The orange glow flickered across his face, glinting off the polished rivets on his leather armor.

"Is something wrong, miss?" he asked. His tone

suggested he hoped the answer was no because "wrong" would mean extra work.

Nyra steeled her resolve. "I need to visit the library."

The guard blinked. "At this hour? It's the middle of the night. Shouldn't you be sleeping?"

"Trust me, I've tried," she replied, voice shaking with the strain of sleeplessness. "When I fall asleep, I can't stay. I want to make use of the time. Please let me go to the library."

He glanced up and down the hallway like he expected a trap. "Councilor Harmond said you're not to wander through the castle unescorted."

She folded her arms. "Then escort me. I'm not asking to roam alone."

"But if the privy councilors find out I let you out of your room in the dead of night..." He grimaced, lowering the torch so it no longer shone directly in her eyes. "They'd have my head for doing something unauthorized. Around here, we don't get sacked for abandoning our post, we get hanged."

Nyra mustered as much empathy as she could, though her frustration simmered. "Technically, I'm your post, not just this room, right?"

The guard peered at her. "I suppose that's right."

"Well, if you're with me then you're not abandoning your post, are you?"

"Are you trying to trick me with words?"

"No, I'm not. Look, if anyone gives you grief, then I promise I will speak to the privy councilors on your behalf," she said. "You can blame me entirely. Tell them I refused to take no for an answer. I will say you had no choice under threat of... well, anything you want."

He let out a long sigh. "Easy for you to say, but I think they'd still hang me for you talking me into letting you out." He stopped a moment, confused by his own attempt at logic. "Anyway, I think you should go back to bed." He paced in front of her door in anxious steps, a soldier weighing the risk of bending the rules. Finally, he paused, turning tired eyes on her. "Look, Miss Nyra, I'm sorry you were dragged into this whole dragon mess, but I don't fancy losing my head. The king and his privy council... they're not exactly lenient with mistakes."

"I'm sorry, I haven't asked your name," Nyra smiled sweetly at him and he narrowed his eyes back at her. Charming him might be harder than she thought. "You know my name, so it's only fair that I know yours."

He still regarded her warily, but he answered nonetheless. "I'm called Thomas."

"Very well, Thomas, let me put it this way: the king wants the curse lifted, yes? That means I need knowledge, and I doubt I'll find it all in my own notes. You'd be helping the entire kingdom by letting me do my research in the library. If the king gets mad at you for helping me, I will remind him that studying is precisely what I'm here to do."

Thomas rubbed his chin. "I suppose... I suppose that might convince them if everything goes wrong."

Her lips twitched into a cautious smile. "Exactly. I give you my word. I will insist it was entirely my idea, and that you only acted out of loyalty to the king's efforts to heal his son. How can they get mad about that?"

He groaned softly, then straightened his back, resolving himself to the gamble. "All right, miss. I'll take you to the library, but on one condition—if we're caught, you speak first, and you better talk fast. If my head winds up on a pike because of you, I'll haunt you for the rest of your life."

"Deal," she said, relieved enough to chuckle under her breath. She'd known ghosts before and, if Thomas was as nice in the afterlife as he was right now, she could handle him.

He gestured for her to wait. He grabbed a torch, withdrew a ring of keys from his belt, and tested the corridor to make sure no other people were around. Then he beckoned her forward. "Follow me. And be quiet. I don't want half the fortress to wake up."

They made their way through several winding halls, each lit by only a few torches. Once, at a corner, he grabbed her arm and pulled her back when he thought he heard footsteps approaching. Both of them froze behind a stone pillar until the faint echo passed. Finally, they arrived at a tall set of double doors bound in iron. A carving above the lintel showed stylized dragons woven in swirling runes. The guard braced himself as he unlocked the door and opened it.

Nyra peered into the darkness, lit only by the Thomas's bobbing torch. The library smelled of dust and old parchment, with a top note of lamp oil. Thomas scurried around the library, lighting enough torches so they could see. Shelves stretched row upon row, teeming with leather-bound tomes and scroll cases. The vaulted ceiling disappeared into gloom. She let out a slow breath, a mix of awe and eager curiosity.

"All right, have a look around," he muttered. "I'll stand guard. The quicker you find your books, the better." His gaze flicked across the looming shelves. "Make it quick, would you? The library always feels a bit haunted to me."

"What is it with you and ghosts?" Nyra teased him as she began looking through the bookshelves.

"My granny, my father's mother, was a crusty old bat," he said. "She was so mean her spirit could not move on after death. She spent years haunting the house I grew up in, and it wasn't fun." He paused a moment, looking embarrassed. "She used hide things from us, and scream like a banshee at all hours of the night."

"Sounds awful."

"It was. You try sleeping with your dead granny screaming in your face all night."

"You try sleeping after you've been forced to leave your home and cure a dragon who doesn't seem to want a cure."

Thomas looked at her and nodded. "Fair point. Get on with it then. We're wasting time talking."

Nyra approached the nearest shelves, scanning titles of massive leather-bound books fastened with metal clasps. Her fingers drifted across spines labeled with archaic symbols. Some, she recognized as references for healing spells and recorded genealogies. Others had elaborate runic titles that made no immediate sense, so she passed them by for the moment.

A narrow table stood at an intersection of rows, topped by a single unlit lantern. She lit it with the guard's torch and set her satchel down. She made notes on scrap of parchment with a bit of charcole.

She found a section labeled "Valendorian Siege Records," which included references to defensive wards used in older military campaigns in a kingdom hundreds of miles away. She pulled out one large book with a cracked leather cover and opened it carefully. Within a few minutes of scanning, she discovered drawings of warding circles once carved into castle foundations to repel enemies. Marginal notes mentioned the use of ritual synergy linking living wards to the fortress's occupants. Though no direct mention of Rhezan's curse appeared, the text hinted that powerful curses or transformations could disrupt such wards.

Next, she discovered an aged grimoire titled "Ancient Curses of the Drakareth Age." It was written in cramped script that required Nyra to run her finger along each line to decipher old Valendorian phrases. She found references to shapeshifting spells that fused draconic magic with mortal blood-magic. The passage told of cursed warriors who gained destructive powers at the cost of their humanity when blood-magic was involved. One phrase caught her eye: "Where mortal blood meets wyrm flame, only sacrifice can unbind." She copied the line onto the parchment scrap, heart pounding with a cautious thrill.

Wyrm. The word carried weight because it was older

than the kingdoms man had carved into the valleys around the mountain, older even than the stones that made up the fortress walls. In the common tongue, people whispered it as another name for dragon, but that was a massive simplification of something fearful and complex.

A wyrm was not merely a beast of scale and fire. Wyrms were elemental, ancient, forged from the raw weave of the world before magic had names or borders. They were intelligence bound in power, memory wrapped in flame. Some could shift between flesh and smoke, between the mortal and the myth. Others, like Rhezan, had once ruled as both, dragon-blooded sovereigns who walked as men but carried fire in their bodies. They could shift, at will, between human and dragon form and, because of this, they were terrifying.

To call someone a wyrm was to speak of legacy, not just biology. It was to name them as part of something vast and dangerous and sacred. And in the forgotten histories Nyra had started to uncover, it was a name that echoed with reverence as much as dread.

From the corner of her eye, she saw Thomas shifting from foot to foot. He huffed and whispered, "How much longer, miss?"

"Not long," she whispered back. "Just... a bit more."

She scanned several more chapters but found only cryptic fragments. One chapter described a ritual requiring the caster's own blood to reinforce or weaken the fortress wards, a direct parallel to the rumors Nyra had heard about blood-magic's unpredictable effects on ancient enchantments. Another told a chilling account of a mage who tried to merge draconic energy with his own soul, resulting in his death and the catastrophic destruction of the entire keep where he lived.

All these stories unsettled Nyra's nerves. She wanted details specifically related to dragon curses, or at least referencing a curse cast on a royal heir. Instead, she gleaned broad warnings about curses that blended mortal and draconic power, plus repeated cautionary tales involving fortress wards turning against their inhabitants if the magic was provoked in the wrong way.

No direct solution revealed itself. However, she found enough to confirm that reversing such a potent curse might require someone to provide a piece of themselves, be it blood or something deeper than that. Although, she didn't immediately know what was deeper or stronger than blood-magic. Her own apprehensions about using forbidden magic nearly choked her, but if her blood was the only path to transformng Rhezan, she would have to muster the courage to broach the subject with the king. She scribbled further notes, forcing her mind to focus.

A clang startled her, and she jumped. Thomas had knocked his shoulder against a corner shelf in his impatience.

"Miss Nyra," he hissed, "the time. We have to get you out of here. One of the other guards might come 'round on patrol, and I don't fancy explaining your presence here."

She glanced up toward a small brass clock near the far side of the library. Its face showed the hour was almost two in the morning. Her body felt numb from the chilly air and hours of tension.

"All right," she said quietly, closing the ancient Drakareth tome. She slipped it back into its spot on the shelf, and memorized the location.

She'd have to come back and read that book again in the daylight. She clutched in her hand the scrap of parchment she'd written upon, then hurried from the library, Thomas leading the way down stillsilent corridors. He kept glancing left and right, as though expecting more guards to materialize and shout "treason" for letting the prisoner out of her room.

When at last they reached Nyra's bedchamber, relief wound tight in her chest. She slipped inside, turning to face Thomas at the threshold. "I meant what I said," she told him. "If anyone discovers what happened tonight, I swear I will take responsibility. In fact, I'll praise you for helping me further my research on behalf of the king."

His mouth twitched, half a smile forming. "I hope you can persuade them as easily as you persuaded me, miss." Then, still fussing, he closed and locked the door.

Nyra stood alone, breath catching in her throat. Her mind buzzed with half-formed theories about fortress wards, curses fueled by draconic flame, and the warnings she had read again and again. Everything pointed toward a single truth: if she wanted the power to unravel Rhezan's curse, she had to walk a razor's edge of forbidden magic without letting the wards of Varynth Hold unravel in the process.

She opened her grimoire, found an empty page at the back, and hastily transferred everything from the piece of parchment into it. She kept thinking about the arcane caution about combining blood-magic with rune-laden wards. The fortress might perceive such an act as a threat and respond with a backlash of suppressed power. Or her blood-magic might just be the key to saving the prince.

She was not sure how Rhezan's father would take that news, or how the fortress might react if she used her blood-magic in a ritual. But she had no illusions about the dangers both magical and political. She could lose more than her freedom if she didn't deliver on lifting the prince's curse.

A dull ache in her eyes finally forced her to rest. She closed the grimoire and massaged her temples. She was cold and bone-weary. Though she felt another surge of frantic need to keep reading, common sense reminded her that she should salvage a few hours of sleep. Her mind had reached its limit for now.

She pulled off her shoes and took off her dressing gown, then sank into the luxurious bed. The sheets felt chilled against her skin at first, but she tugged the covers around her shoulders, letting exhaustion creep in. She pictured the glimmer of Rhezan's golden eyes, that brief spark of fury mixed with something akin to desperation. His temper was as threatening as the fortress wards themselves, and she would have to face both soon.

Nyra inhaled slowly, summoning a thread of courage. She thought of the cryptic line she copied down: "Where mortal blood meets wyrm flame, only sacrifice can unbind." The words echoed in her mind, as though carved into the darkness. Would it be her sacrifice, or Rhezan's that would be required? She really had no clue, and the only thing she knew for certain was that more risk lay ahead.

Her eyelids finally grew too heavy to keep open. The tension in her body melted, and she allowed a faint flicker of hope to soothe her anxiety. She clutched the memory of her findings resolved that, come daylight, she would be one step closer to discovering a method to calm Rhezan's fire before it consumed them both.

At last, her breathing slowed. Her mind drifted toward restless dreams of runic wards and roaring flames. In that uncertain realm between waking and slumber, she steeled herself for the days to come. She would have to contend with an embittered prince, unearth the missing pieces of a centuries-old curse, and tread ever so carefully around a monarchy that distrusted her forbidden magic. Yet something deeper than fear urged her forward—a promise she had made to heal, whether the kingdom accepted her methods or not.

CHAPTER

FIVE

Nyra woke to soft gray light filtering through the window in her chamber. At first, she thought she might return to the restless sleep that had plagued her throughout the night after the trip to the library. Instead, she forced herself up, remembering that the guards would come to wake her sooner rather than later. The sudden swirl of anxiety in her stomach pushed aside any tempting thought of lying back down.

She washed with cold water from the basin, trying to gather composure. Then she slipped into a plain olive-green dress from the wardrobe and belted it at the waist. She glanced at a mirror set within a polished steel frame. Though she could not see her reflection well, she could tell her hair was messy from tossing and turning on her pillow. She tried to smooth it as best she could, placing a few stray locks behind her ears. The faint bruise-like shadows beneath her eyes told the story of her sleepless night.

A timid steward appeared at her door to escort her to breakfast. The man gave a terse bow before leading her into the dim corridors. Thomas followed behind them. The corridor opened into a tall stone threshold leading into the Great Hall, which was lavishly appointed. The ceiling soared high overhead, supported by thick rafters and etched pillars. Firelight from a massive hearth on one side glowed across the polished stone floors. Conversation among those already gathered in the hall dropped into murmurs the instant she appeared. She sensed many gazes turning her way.

She spotted the king at the head table. King Vorian stood as she approached, motioning for her to sit beside him. She hesitated for only a moment, feeling entirely out of place among the gilded chairs and embroidered table runners. Yet she forced herself forward, crossing the open space with measured steps. Her heartbeat thudded in her ears.

When she arrived at the table, the king's dark eyes fixed on her. He inclined his head in polite greeting. "Good morning, Nyra," he said. His tone was kind, though weighed down by something too heavy to define as mere tiredness.

She bobbed a curtsey, hoping she did it right. "Your Majesty."

He gestured to the seat on his right. She sank onto the padded chair, acutely conscious of the hush that rolled across the tables where nobles and privy councilors sat. Servants came forward, placing fresh bread, fruit, and bowls of warm porridge before her. The aroma of cinnamon and cloves drifted up, momentarily distracting her from the tension. She had eaten very little the night before, so her body craved food even as apprehension knotted her muscles.

King Vorian lowered himself onto his seat again. Others resumed their own conversations in quiet murmurs, though Nyra sensed a great many of them still watched her. The king leaned closer to her, his voice meant only for her ears. "I trust your chamber was comfortable. Did you sleep well?"

Nyra smoothed a hand along the front of her dress. "It was... comfortable enough, sire." A bittersweet sting churned inside her chest. Comfort did not matter if she felt trapped, but she kept that thought to herself.

He nodded as though he expected her polite reply. "Please, eat a little." He gestured toward her plate. "You will need strength to deal with my son."

She took a spoonful of porridge, found it sweetened with honey and spiced fruit, and swallowed quickly, uncertain how long the food would stay down. Her stomach was already gone queasy when she realized the king's gaze remained steady on her.

After a few measured spoonfuls of porridge, he spoke again. "My councilors have told me about your talents. They say your healing powers saved a man from Fogrot with surprising ease. Your gift is what we need here."

Nyra forced herself to meet his eyes. "I was only doing what I was taught by my mother and grandmother, sir."

He allowed a small, sad smile. "Humility. That is commendable." He paused for a moment, letting the clash of silverware and the murmur of distant talk hover like a backdrop to their private conversation. "What do you think of our fortress, Miss Nyra?"

She studied his face. She sensed he already guessed her answer. "It is impressive, sir. But it is very different from what I am used to."

A flicker of understanding passed across his features. "Yes, the Drakareth Mountains can be quite hard on those who grew up in gentler lands."

He went silent then, as if choosing his next words. A pair of servants brought carafes of hot spiced tea and poured a measure for both Nyra and the king before stepping back. She took a small sip, bracing herself for what she suspected would be a more serious discussion.

King Vorian leaned closer, enough that she could see slight lines of exhaustion around his eyes. "Forgive my bluntness, Miss Nyra, but I must speak plainly. Our realm stands on the brink of something dire. My son's affliction has weakened us more than many outside these walls can imagine. If Rhezan cannot regain his human form, then I do not have an heir who can continue our bloodline. Rival kingdoms wait like wolves, eager to pounce at the slightest sign that my royal lineage will die with me."

Nyra's heart nearly skipped a beat. Was the weight of the entire kingdom's fate on her shoulders? If so, then she was in a precarious position, indeed. She swallowed and set her cup down. "I understand your concern, Your Majesty, but... I have not been able to do anything yet with the prince. He refuses to talk with me. He thinks I'm a fraud and there is no help for him."

The king's gaze shifted momentarily, as if he took no pleasure in cornering her. "Rhezan has grown bitter over the years. I cannot fault him for that. Countless healers and mages have tried and failed to lift his curse. Not one has succeeded. He sees them as charlatans but, in truth, it is only fear that we may never be able to restore him that drives his fury. He may well see you as an enemy, for now, but I have every confidence that you can break through his defences."

"You do? That's a lovely sentiment but I don't share your confidence. I can't guarantee that he will let me work with him and, even if he does, I can't guarantee that anything I do will work."

He spread his hands lightly on the table. "But, you see, I must insist that you do break this curse on my son." His voice was ragged with emotion, and Nyra's heart almost broke for him. "My kingdom is in peril. Without an heir in human form who can sire more heirs, then our kingdom will be conquered by the enemies who even now wait at the gate for just one opportunity to strike. Whether it is fair or not to compel you to do this no longer matters. War will come if he remains a dragon, and the whole land will suffer for it."

Nyra pressed her lips together. She was angry at being forced into this situation, but if the king wasn't just blowing smoke, then war in the land would reach her village sooner rather than later, and the thought terrified her.

"What if he won't listen to me? I can't help someone who doesn't want to be helped."

"Let me talk with him. I guarantee he will cooperate when I am finished with him."

"He made it clear he wanted me gone. And, forgive me, Your Majesty, but he is a dragon. How can you convince him to let me help?"

The king listened quietly. He glanced out over the other tables, the hush in the Great Hall still conspicuous. She wondered if everyone was waiting for a cue to start speaking normally. Several councilors cast cautious looks her way.

King Vorian turned back to her. "I am still his father, and he is still my son. Once, he possessed a heart large enough to fill this entire hall with laughter. He was a poet and a musician as well as a fine soldier. If you had seen Rhezan before the curse, you would scarcely recognize him as the same being who lurks in those caverns below us now." His eyes shone with tears. "I will convince him to let you in. But you must earn his trust."

Something about the king's voice—so gentle and pained—made Nyra's chest tighten. She pictured the rage in Rhezan's golden eyes and tried to reconcile that image with a version of the man she never knew. It seemed impossible that the dragon prince could have been kind and joyful. Yet sorrow weighed heavily on the king's words, and it was not a sorrow feigned for political advantage. She could sense the heartbreak of a father trying to save his lost child.

She let out an unsteady breath. "I... cannot imagine Rhezan that way," she admitted softly. "He was so hostile and terrifying when I met him."

A series of faint creases lined King Vorian's brow. "Think of his fury as a wall he built to protect himself from disappointment. Every time a promised cure failed, he lost faith in our ability to save him. I cannot fully blame him for that bitterness. But I must beg you, give him a chance and do not give up."

Nyra blinked. The sour taste in her mouth deepened. She set her spoon aside and clasped her hands in her lap. "I cannot promise anything more but this: I will try my best." She struggled to put her frustration into words without sounding insolent. "But he must let me in. I cannot work with him if he continues to shut me out." She paused a moment, weighing her words, wondering if they would be understood or get her hanged.

If Thomas was to be believed, the chances of getting hanged outweighed any understanding she might find for speaking her mind. She decided to chance it anyway. "It's not easy to do my best work knowing when I feel so trapped."

The king's expression softened. "That is understandable. We didn't give you a choice, and I wish there had been another way, but..." He hesitated, picking his next words carefully. "I could not risk you saying no. No one else has been able to help my son. Councilor Jori insists you have the skill to succeed where others failed. He and the other councilors see something in you. I hope it is true."

She glanced at her hands. A wave of old guilt rose, thinking of the secret and forbidden art she kept hidden from the world. She was not certain she would find any bright solution in these cold halls. Yet the sincerity in King Vorian's eyes made her want to try. If her mother's memory could guide her, maybe there was a chance, no matter how small.

Across the hall, a cluster of courtiers flicked their gazes toward her, then quickly looked down at their plates. Clearly, curiosity about her conversation with the king was high. She felt no comfort in their stares.

King Vorian gently reached out until his fingers brushed the back of her hand, a brief paternal gesture. "Try. That is all I ask of you. Rhezan was gentle once. He was good and gracious to people. He is not past saving. My boy is still in there, suffocating beneath all that anger and heartbreak."

Nyra's throat tightened at the subtle plea in his voice. She had not expected such raw humanity behind that regal facade. He seemed more a grieving father than a calculating monarch, though she recognized he was, in essence, both.

"If you can see the man inside the dragon, maybe he will sense your sincerity. Maybe that will lower his walls enough for you to do your work," King Vorian said quietly. "He is not cruel at his core, though he may appear so now. I swear that to you."

She inhaled slowly, letting his words sink in. She believed that he believed it. The recollection of Rhezan's furious roar made her stomach clench, yet a spark of empathy flickered within her. She tried to imagine how many times the prince had endured spells, potions, rituals... all failures. Failure must have tasted like ashes to a proud soul. Sheltered behind his rage, he likely found it easier to snarl than to hope. For a moment, she thought of how her own fear might mirror his hopelessness, each of them bound by the fortress's demands. Perhaps that was the place to begin.

She set her hand lightly on the table beside her half-eaten meal. Her mind churned through everything the king had said. When she finally spoke, her voice wavered. "I am frightened. I do not lie. But I will not give up, if there is any chance at all to help him. I only ask that you know how difficult it is for me—"

King Vorian nodded gravely, interrupting her with a soft sigh. "You have my understanding. And you have whatever resources you need. You may not move beyond these walls, but every volume in the library is at your disposal. Take what herbs you need from the storerooms. Command a steward to gather fresh supplies for your potions. I will ensure no one hinders you." His tone shifted, turning urgent. "Time is against us. If I do not convince the world I still have a human heir soon, the other kingdoms will attack. I will talk to him. Convince him to work with you."

Nyra peered around the room, noticing how the courtiers' conversations grew uneasy again as they watched her talk with the king. A chill touched her arms, despite the warmth of the fire. She pictured the lines of men with lances capable of shooting dragons out of the sky.

She pictured war-torn fields with people fleeing so that a king might preserve his throne. She felt the tension rising like an invisible tide. This was not some trivial family feud. It was the fate of an entire kingdom at stake. She clenched her hands tightly together.

She lifted her gaze back to King Vorian. "I understand, Your Majesty." Her voice came out steadier now, though her throat felt tight. "I promise I will do everything I can to help Prince Rhezan. I will not withdraw simply because he pushes me away. I only wish I had a clearer idea of how to break his curse."

CHAPTER
SIX

When Nyra received word that the king had spoken with his son, she gathered her grimoire and supplies and, with Thomas as her escort, descended into the caverns, following the markings on the walls that were as much a warning about the dragon as signposts for finding him. It felt colder today. She pulled her woolen cape tighter around her shoulders, bracing against the chill that crept through Varynth Hold's deepest passageways. Morning light didn't reach this far, and even the wall-mounted torches barely dented the heavy gloom pressing in around her.

She passed two guards stationed at an archway, their expressions grim, though they made no move to stop her. She clutched her satchel, wishing fervently that she had brought the thicker gloves left behind in her chamber.

She followed the winding path that led to the cavern where Prince Rhezan spent most of his time. Crossing the threshold, Nyra inhaled a breath of cold, mineral-laced air.

The chamber was enormous, full of towering pillars of rock and echoes that carried each footstep in gentle waves. Flickers of torchlight revealed the slightest sheen on the walls, remnants of old enchantments etched in patterns she was only partly able to decipher.

Toward the back, Rhezan's form sprawled across the smoothed stone floor. The sight of him momentarily stole her breath. His dragon frame was massive, muscles coiled beneath obsidian scales that looked almost wet in the dim light. A faint glow along their edges shimmered a deep crimson at every slow rise and fall of his flank.

Nyra's boots scraped softly as she approached. She forced herself not to shrink away from the fierce outline of his horns or the white slivers of his curved talons. She could not forget how easily he could slice through stone or belch flame if provoked. But in this moment, he looked exhausted.

She paused a short distance from him. The cold numbed her fingers even though she wore gloves. "It's colder today than usual," she offered quietly.

His thick tail shifted, and she tried not to flinch. For a moment, she believed he might ignore her altogether. Then his massive head lifted, and she found herself pinned by his golden draconic stare. His eyes glowed with faint embers in the darkness. She resisted the urge to step back.

"What do you want?" The words echoed like low thunder against the cavern walls.

"I—well...your father said he spoke with you." She wet

her lips, the dryness of her throat mocking her attempt to speak calmly. "I wanted to see if you were... all right."

His snort stirred a cloud of dust. "All right. That is an odd thing to ask a cursed man."

Nyra's grip on her satchel strap tightened. She willed herself to calm down. Somewhere, water dripped in a steady rhythm, punctuating the tension with every drop. "I know you do not trust me, but if I am to help you then we must get to work. Your father says your enemies will attack if you are not—"

"Human," he finished for her, flashing his massive teeth at her. "Yes, I am well aware of the political state of things."

"Then, you agree we must work together to lift the curse as quickly as we can?"

He lifted the ridges above his eyes, a quiet assessment in that gaze. "Do not mistake agreement that my father is right with enthusiasm for the process," he said. "I do not think you can help me at all but, by all means, let us do the will of the king."

The torchlight flickered over his scales, highlighting the spots where tension lined his shoulders. Nyra noticed the subtle trembling when he stretched his foreleg, as though some unseen strain weighed on him. She felt a twist of concern. She had read about shapeshifting curses draining energy, leaving the inflicted mind fatigued. She wondered if this was what she saw before her.

She dared another step forward, ignoring how the cold made her teeth threaten to chatter. "This place is freezing," she said quietly. "The Great Hall is better heated. It might help if we—"

His tail lashed in a quick, irritated arc. She expected him to snap at her or demand that she leave, but he exhaled instead, releasing a rough, steaming breath onto the stone floor. "The Great Hall," he repeated. "You think I can stroll in there at this size?"

Nyra straightened her posture. "Well—no, not at this size. That was why I suggested we might find a different place to talk."

"A different place," Rhezan echoed, some edge of mockery in his voice. "Yes, humans love to talk in comfortable spots."

He did not move for a few seconds, and she debated whether to risk pressing further. But then she saw a peculiar shift in his expression, as if he had decided something. He lowered his head slightly, and she felt the oddest flutter of magic swelling around them. It made the hair on her arms stand on end.

She took a step back, instinct warning her of oncoming power. The air turned charged, dense with the taste of arcane energy. Rhezan's scales rippled, and the sight was both breathtaking and disturbing as shadows rolled along his body as if the darkness itself was folding inward. His towering frame began to contract, limbs drawing closer to his body, wings shrinking against his back. Bones seemed to rearrange under the surface of his scales. The entire cavern resonated with a tangible hum.

Nyra pressed a hand over her mouth. Part of her wanted to run, a primal fear whispering that watching with a dragon's shapeshifting might be dangerous. What if he involuntarily breathed fire as he grew smaller? Yet she forced herself to remain still, mesmerized as his transformation despite her fear.

At last, the wave of magic subsided. Two-thirds of his customary size, he crept toward her on all fours. He was now the approximate size of a small elephant. He shuddered, letting out a ragged sigh. A fine sheen of sweat glistened along the ridges of his neck, and his breath came in heavy bursts.

She stepped toward him carefully, not daring to rest a hand on his scales. Up close, she saw how heavily he was breathing. "Does... does it hurt?" she asked, voice gently wavering with sympathy.

"Everything about this curse hurts," he replied, half-lidding his eyes. He lingered, as if regaining balance. Then, with a frustrated grunt, he swung his head in the direction of the arched doorway. "Let us go, then. You wanted the Great Hall's fire. We will see if your comfort truly makes any difference in how you work."

Nyra nodded, astounded that he was willing to move somewhere more open, somewhere that reminded him of the life he could not fully live. The king must have had one hell of a talk with him. Their footsteps echoed unevenly, her boots scraping the stone while his claws clicked in quiet staccato. She kept glancing at him, noticing faint twitches in his limbs, as if the forced shapeshift had a draining effect. Her heart twisted in her chest.

In the corridors, servants scrambled out of their path the instant they saw Rhezan. One of them pressed her back into the wall. The other did the same but closed his eyes as they passed, probably thinking if he didn't see the dragon the dragon wouldn't see him, like a child hiding behind the drapes. Rhezan cast them no more than a passing glance at them, though Nyra caught the stiff set of his jaw, bitterness hidden beneath his stoic facade.

They emerged onto the main floor, the path opening into the broad corridor leading to the Great Hall. Tall torches flanked the carved entrance. The flickering flames chased away some of the gloom. Beyond, she heard the low murmur of conversations, presumably from a few staff preparing midday tasks.

Rhezan curved his neck, peering in. He looked uneasy, almost vulnerable. Nyra's breath hitched at the flicker of his golden eyes reflecting uncertainty instead of anger. Then, as if steeling himself, he walked inside.

The Great Hall's arches soared overhead. A tapestry of the royal crest draped the far wall, its golden threads lit by the large central hearth near the back. Nyra approached the fireplace, and beckoned to him. He followed at a measured pace, though she could sense his reluctance in every step. Servants scattered into corners or found sudden work that took them elsewhere.

Stopping before the fire, she felt the warmth spread across her numb nose and cheeks. She sighed, letting her stiff shoulders relax. The stone tiles, though blackened by centuries of soot, looked newly swept. Though the Hall was mostly empty, Nyra felt the charged silence that signaled everyone's attention was firmly on them. The presence of a dragon here was probably unusual, especially now.

Awkwardly, she glanced at Rhezan, unsure of what to say or do. He lowered his body onto his haunches, tail curled around him. His wings folded tight, as though he did not wish to impose more than he already did. She stifled a pang of empathy.

"Thank you for agreeing to move," she said. "You have no clue how cold it felt down there."

He huffed, a soft sound of mild acknowledgment. "You humans. Always grumbling about the temperature."

She tried a small smile, though she doubted he noticed. The fire crackled, sending gentle embers dancing upward. For a while, neither of them spoke. She wondered if it was wise to remain silent, or if she should offer some conversation that might help him relax.

"Tell me something," Rhezan said. "My father insists you have magic that can help me. Magic that others have deemed forbidden. I've heard whispers between the guards and the servants—my hearing is quite keen, you see—about the kind of power you wield. These rumors are not...complimentary. What kind of magic do you possess?"

She inhaled slowly, reminding herself not to appear defensive. "Blood-magic," she whispered, afraid servants passing by the room might hear. "I learned it from my mother, long ago before she died." She paused, uncertain how much she should reveal. "Blood-magic amplifies any spell by channeling the user's will through the lifeforce in their blood. It is not all about violence or corruption; however, some people believe that is its only purpose."

"I know what blood-magic is." His gaze flickered, curiosity and doubt mingling in those golden eyes, though he didn't seem to be surprised that she was a blood-magic healer. "I am not stupid. Blood is powerful. I have felt its pull within the runes throughout the fortress. These are the wards that help protect Varynth Hold from attacks. But our laws forbid your kind of magic. Yet you propose to use it on me?"

"I have no idea if I'll need to employ blood-magic to lift your curse," Nyra admitted. "But some things cannot be undone by conventional spells or rituals. My mother believed that if one intends no harm, and if the blood is offered willingly, it can be used to save lives rather than destroy them."

"That is not what the stories say," Rhezan said. He eyed her from the corner of his vision, tension shifting in his loin as he adjusted his stance closer to the fire. "Stories say blood-mages twisted spells into weapons. They nearly sank entire strongholds into the earth at one point. Creatures with that talent are not to be trusted."

Nyra shot him a stony look. The heat at her back felt like a shield, helping her gather resolve. "I am not a creature. I do know the stories paint anyone like me as evil. I have spent my life trying to prove that my powers can be a force for good. People have called me monstrous too, Prince Rhezan, though all I have ever done was heal or protect people."

He did not reply at once. His reptilian eyes swept over her, as if searching for cracks in her sincerity. She lingered at arm's length from his lowered snout. Every flick of his tail reminded her that even at two-thirds size, he was dangerously strong. Still, her heart ached for him in ways she scarcely understood.

After a moment, he shifted, a subtle movement that caused the scales around his throat to ripple. "And how have you used your powers to heal your patients?"

"I've treated festering wounds that no potion could touch—sealed them with my own blood when I had to," Nyra said, her voice low but steady. "There was a child once, barely breathing from moonfever. I brought him back. And there was an old man cursed so badly that his mind had splintered. I held him together long enough to lift it. I've helped mothers give birth when the midwives had given up. And I spent three nights fighting a death-curse that wrapped itself around a hunter like smoke." She smiled at him. "I have some experience with hopeless situations."

He gave a low rumble that sounded almost like approval. The tension in his posture slackened just enough for her to sense that he might be listening more openly. "And you've never lost a patient?"

The smile on her face faded. "I have. And each loss is seared into my brain so that I will never forget. But more often than not, my patients survive."

Rhezan inclined his head a fraction as he peered at her. For a moment, his large golden eyes were unnerving. "You truly care about people, then?"

Nyra swallowed hard. If anyone else had questioned her motives, she would've put them in their place. But there was something so vulnerable in his question, she decided to answer earnestly. "I do," she said quietly. "No matter what the law says about blood-magic, I would not condemn someone to pain or death if I have the ability to heal them. So... yes, I care." Her voice faltered for an instant. "That includes you. You are no less deserving of healing."

For a heartbeat, the hall felt utterly silent, and she was afraid she had overstepped. Then she saw a haunted flicker in his eyes, something raw that she had not seen before. Briefly, it made her think of the sorrow King Vorian had described, the combination of heartbreak and betrayal that had turned Rhezan into a guarded, distant figure.

His next words confirmed it. "You spoke about your mother. If she was anything like you, she must have been formidable," he said. He stared into the flames, his voice nearly lost under the crackle of the logs. "My mother was formidable, too. And tender and loving. When I was small, she sang lullabies that carried through these corridors. Wherever I roamed, her voice felt like safety."

Nyra's chest tightened. She had not expected such a confession. She dared not interrupt as he continued.

"She died too soon. In childbirth with my brother who did not survive." His tail shifted across the tiles, scraping softly. "My father cared for me after that. It wasn't always easy." Something passed over his face, half-sadness, half-anger. "I suppose that was the first time I learned the truth of how easily happiness can be torn away."

Feeling her heart twist, Nyra cautiously said, "Your mother sounds lovely."

Rhezan gave a bitter snort. "Yes, she was. Our people would have done anything for their queen. And that was why her death shook all of us to our core. Grief can be as cruel as any blade." He paused, exhaling a breath that caused a wan glow of heat in the air around them.

His voice was sharp, and she felt the deep hurt in every word. She wished there was something comforting to say. Instead, she just remained still, letting him see the sympathy in her eyes.

"Many mages and healers tried to lift this curse," he said in a low tone. "They came to me with spells and potions and rituals. They all failed. And so you come here, another in a line of healers, speaking about your blood-magic. Yet I stand no closer to freedom, caged in these halls or forced to lurk in the caverns below like the vile beast that I am."

"Even though every prior attempt has failed you, it does not mean all future attempts are doomed to failure. I promised your father that I will do everything I can to help you. I make you the same promise now."

She yearned to reach out a hand and rest it softly on his scaled forearm, offering some measure of solace. Instinct, however, told her that any contact until she had earned his trust would be going too far. His posture had tensed again, ridges rising around his neck. The ephemeral moment of closeness was slipping away. She watched his jaw set, anger or frustration chasing away the vulnerability she had glimpsed.

He pushed his hindquarters up, stepping back from the hearth. The action startled her, and she stilled, her heart pounding. His narrowed gaze told her the moment of empathy was done.

"This is pointless," he snapped, voice turning cold. "You will waste your time searching for a miracle that does not exist. Do you imagine your blood alone will undo this cursed magic? You have healed humans before but have you ever transformed a beast into a human?"

She opened her mouth, though she was not sure how to answer. "I—"

"That's what I thought," Rhezan growled, lashing his tail once across the floor, scattering a few loose pieces of firewood. The clattering sounds made the few onlookers shrink away even more. "I agreed to allow you to try helping me, but if you think my father will allow you to use blood-magic, I think you're going to be disappointed."

"I think your father will do whatever it takes to turn you human again. I think you underestimate him. And me."

He scoffed, a flare of heated breath escaping his nostrils. "I am a realist. If you truly wish to help me then do so by acknowledging you might fail, too. You will learn that some curses cannot be undone." His voice cracked, though he tried to mask it with a snarl. "Just spare me your compassion. It will make no difference to me."

He turned abruptly, pacing toward the corridor that led back to his domain. Nyra watched helplessly, her throat tight. The massive door creaked under the push of his shoulder. Then, with a swift burst of movement, he was gone, trailing bitterness in his wake. She remained by the hearth, the warmth feeling strangely hollow now.

Servants peered from behind the archways, uncertain if she needed assistance. She forced small nods to reassure them before gathering her satchel. Her legs felt heavy as she left the Great Hall, each step echoing like the remnants of a shattered conversation.

Back in her own chamber, she closed the door against the corridor's gloom. Candlelight flickered over the curved wooden panels, and for a moment she simply stood there, collecting her breath. She had seen the man behind his anger for one fleeting moment, only for that fragile closeness to vanish. Sliding her satchel onto the table, she suppressed the ache that weighed on her chest.

"Think," she muttered to herself, willing away the cold dread that threatened to creep in. She needed to dive deeper into the texts that spoke about shapeshifting curses. The fortress library held more volumes on metamorphosis and wards, though many might be cryptic. She had to find them, study them, perhaps uncover a portion of the puzzle that others had overlooked. Her mind churned with the memory of Rhezan's expression when he mentioned his mother. There was a lost and battered soul beneath those scales.

SEVEN

Nyra woke to a thin light creeping in around the heavy drapes covering her bedchamber's lone window. The morning chill pressed against her skin as she rose from the plush bed. Although it was more comfortable than any place she had ever slept, the fortress's cold stone and her own restless thoughts made slumber feel anything but restful. She shivered as she pulled her dressing gown over her linen shift. The fire in the grate was burning brightly, but it had only been lit an hour ago by a chambermaid, and the majority of the room was still cold.

She knocked on her bedchamber door, the signal to the guards that she was ready to leave. When the thick wooden door opened, she found Thomas waiting outside, as usual. Two other guards, Gareth and Julian, had taken most of the night watches outside her room. She was on a friendly, first-name basis with all of her jailers, and they all seemed to genuinely like her. It seemed to make the prisoner experience a little less daunting.

"Good morning, Thomas. I see you have the day watch with me. I hope you're well?"

"As well as can be expected, my lady," he replied. Nyra liked that they'd all taken to calling her 'my lady' like she was someone noble and important. She wasn't about to let it go to her head. She knew that it might take only one wrong step to land her in the dungeons or, worse yet, inhabiting one of the caves near Rhezan's. It was best to keep her feet firmly on the ground.

"After I break my fast, I must go to Prince Rhezan," she told Thomas. "He can't ignore or stall me every day. I'm sure his father wouldn't like that."

He offered her a quick nod, his expression tinged with something akin to apology. "The prince has left the castle," he said quietly, shifting his weight from one foot to the other. "He flew off early this morning. He did not say anything to anyone, just took wing."

Nyra's heart dropped. "He left? Why would he do such a thing?"

Thomas gave her a one-shouldered shrug. "He goes flying whenever his temper runs high. It seems to help him cool off. Problem is, there are villagers in the valleys below this mountain who have Sky Lances."

"What in the world is that?"

"A machine with the sole purpose of killing dragons. The nearby villages built them after Prince Rhezan was cursed. He doesn't seem to fear them when he's off flying, but I think he should. His Royal Highness seems to have a bit of a death wish, if you ask me."

Nyra rested a hand on the stone corridor wall. She had heard rumors before about dragon-killing weapons but she had never seen one and, to be honest, hadn't really cared about them until now. The images she had conjured in her mind were unsettling enough, but Thomas's explanation cemented the threat.

"Sky Lances," she echoed. "They are enormous trebuchet-like contraptions, right? Capable of launching enormous spears?"

Thomas nodded. "They have enough force to shoot a dragon from the sky. No one has used them here in a long while, but enough remain in the outlying towns, and that makes the king nervous."

Nyra glanced down the corridor, her thoughts drifting. If Rhezan's temper had driven him away, she could only guess what turmoil haunted him. Her attempts to see past his anger had ended in guarded conversations. Now he was gone, and she did not know for how long. She pressed her fingers together to still an anxious tremor. "Does the king know?"

"The king was informed. The privy counilors always say the prince will return when he needs to. Anyway, I am here to see to your safety and comfort," Thomas said, offering a weak grin. "I've even acquired permission for you to visit the library any time, day or night."

She grinned at him. "Well, that's something, at least. You won't have to worry about losing your head the next time I want to read in the middle of the night."

"Yes, my lady. I feel much better about it." He gave her a goofy grin and suddenly seemed much younger than she thought he was.

Thomas was lanky and broad-shouldered, with a mop of brown hair that never quite stayed tucked beneath his helm. He had chiseled jawline and kind eyes that crinkled when he smiled, usually a little too quickly, like someone eager to be liked. Though he carried a sword at his side and wore the king's colors with pride, there was a nervous energy about him, the sort that suggested he was still getting used to the idea of being a soldier at all. When he grinned, boyish and a little crooked, he looked barely older than eighteen.

"I am glad,' Nyra replied. "I appreciate the news about the prince. Has he... done this often of late?"

"More times than I can count," Thomas replied. "Before you arrived, he had been gone for nearly two weeks. Eventually, he returns, though he still seems to be as sullen as when he left. I understand he carries a great, sorrowful weight, but it is risky for him to fly out in the open." He paused, raking a hand through his hair. "It's a small mercy that he doesn't often return to us injured."

Nyra's eyes widened. "But he has been injured before?"

Thomas gave her a look that hinted at regret that he alarmed her. "Minor scrapes, my lady. Nothing serious... yet."

Nyra swallowed a pang of worry. It cut deeper than she expected, imagining him alone in the wide skies, targeted by lethal war machines from every village that feared dragons. "There is nothing we can do until he returns, I suppose?"

"Not unless we want to chase him with crossbows. Which, trust me, I do not," Thomas said, flustered. He waved a hand, as though brushing away the image. "He will come back. We just have to wait for him to be done flying."

Nyra thanked him quietly, then ducked back into her chamber to dress. She layered warmer garments—a plain wool tunic under a thicker robe—before emerging into the corridor once more. With Rhezan gone, there was no immediate opportunity to continue her attempts at counteracting his curse. Sitting idle and fretting would achieve nothing. She decided she would visit the library.

A short while later, she made her way through the fortress's winding passages, Thomas trailing a few paces behind. Varynth Hold felt more oppressive in Rhezan's absence, its echoing corridors colder, as if losing the presence of its chief occupant drained a certain vital spark from the stones. She pulled her robe close while the austere torchlight flickered across the walls. Servants passed in silence, heads bowed, either unconcerned or well-practiced in concealing any fear they might hold.

Upon entering the library, Nyra drew a calming breath. The familiar scent of parchment and lamp oil always soothed her. Immense shelves lined the tall chamber, crammed with heavy tomes and brittle scrolls. She approached an unoccupied table near the back, set her satchel down, and exhaled slowly.

She pulled notes from her earlier research from her

bag: lists of ingredients, half-translated runic diagrams, theoretical cures that combined blood-magic with protective wards. She had begun to piece these findings together like fragments of a puzzle, but large gaps remained.

She spent the morning reviewing each text she could find that mentioned transformations, curses, or shapeshifting. Few works gave clear instructions. In some, the runic references suggested that any magical synergy depended heavily on powerful catalysts to spark the runes to work. Emberleaf was mentioned repeatedly, far more often than the others: wyrmroot, silverthorn bark, ghost-bloom petals, and ashvine sap. She had encountered all of them in her late-night readings, but Emberleaf's consistent appearance across sources caught her attention. Perhaps it wasn't just one of many components. It looked like it might be a key ingredient.

Eventually, she rubbed at her eyes, scanning a passage that described binding and severing mortal-and-dragon souls using complicated herb mixtures, runes, and incantations that demanded an immense amount of magical energy. She had lost track of time until Councilor Harmond came into the library. Thomas, who had been leaning against a bookshelf on the far side of the room, quickly straightened up. Nyra had been around long enough to know that slouching around one's superiors would be a good reason to get dressed down.

Without waiting for her to speak, Harmond rested both palms on the table and cleared his throat. "We heard from the stewards that you have compiled a list of required materials. His Majesty wants to assure you every attempt will be made to secure what you need."

Nyra forced a polite smile, though her nerves were frayed beneath. "Yes, I have been gathering references. Some of these items are extremely rare. I am not sure how feasible it is to gather them all. I would also like to know if anything can be found locally in the mountains."

The councillor shook his head slowly. "Our staff has scoured the slopes for centuries for herbs and plants. If it is out there, we will find it."

"These are the things I need." She turned her notes around so he could see them, and he dragged a finger down the page as he read. When he read about Emberleaf, he stopped at looked at her.

"This herb does not grow on the mountain. In fact, several of these ingredients cannot be sourced locally. We can supply all manner of standard ingredients, but for these exotic requests, we must rely on trade."

A flicker of hope drained from Nyra's face. "Then it depends on the supply caravans that travel throughout the kingdom?"

"Exactly so," he replied. "The MerChain caravans are due through the valley within the month. When they arrive, we will send servants down into the villages to collect what you need."

"It would be much better if I went myself. I'm not sure the servants will know what I'm looking for."

Harmond's eyes crinkled as he smiled. "Admirable try to get out of the castle, but no. You will remain here. The king will simply buy out everything you need. You should know, however, that with tensions rising in the east, especially near Desmir, our trade routes have been hindered on occasion. The Lords of Desmir want to see if the rumors that Prince Rhezan is unfit to rule are true, so they hold any caravan they think might have information until they're certain the traders have no information to share." He paused, as if weighing how much to share. "We are not at war, but they are exploiting our perceived vulnerability."

Nyra bit her lip. The thought that politics could now block her from the very resources needed to heal Rhezan made her sick to her stomach. "If we have difficulty importing anything I might need for the rituals, that means I might not even be able to start preparing a cure."

He inclined his head. "Rest assured that we will find what you need. We have connections in other regions. It may take longer, and it will be more expensive, but the king will pay whatever it costs." His tone remained free of hostility, but the undercurrent of urgency was unmistakable.

Nyra sank onto the bench at the table. She had believed from the start that every solution might demand unimaginable effort. Hearing the details of supply routes being blocked brought the reality of that difficulty crashing down. "I will keep looking," she said. "Perhaps there is an alternative. One that does not require quite so many rare components."

The councillor offered a perfunctory nod and departed. Thomas eased over, his expression troubled. "I listened to all that. Sounds complicated."

She closed one of the dusty tomes and stared at its blank leather cover. "More than complicated. We have half a dozen prime ingredients blocked by trading embargoes or suspicious border checks. I fear by the time they arrive, war could erupt even sooner than we think it might."

Thomas's eyes darted around, checking for eavesdroppers. "You heard what the councillor said, though. The king will not let the supply lines fail. He will do everything he can to get you what you need."

"Perhaps." She forced herself to inhale slowly and not let panic claim her. Then, setting her jaw, she reached for her parchment and quill. "I will refine the list. If I can reduce the number of exotic ingredients, maybe that will help."

"And if those ingredients are the very ones you need?"

"Then I guess I'm as stuck waiting for supplies as I am for my patient to return from his flying."

Nyra spent the rest of that day hunting references among the shelves, with Thomas occasionally helping bring stepstools so she could reach higher volumes. Though he sometimes bemoaned the risk of punishment if the librarians discovered him fussing with the restricted section, he offered assistance. His uneasy attempts at humor, the comments about "getting strung up by my ankles for messing with the old archives" provided fleeting smiles that eased her tension.

As evening approached, she closed the grimoire she was reading and pushed aside her notes. Her back ached from leaning over the table, yet relief was not forthcoming. The pile of advanced texts had yielded only more permutations of the same spells. They all demanded potent catalysts. She jotted an updated list on a single sheet: Emberleaf, ashvine sap, heartsbud, and a few other obscure items whose existence was uncertain. The scope of her request made her head spin.

She left the library with Thomas at her side. Anxiety gnawed at her thoughts as she wandered through the fortress corridors toward her room. A solitary supper sat waiting in her chamber: roast chicken, root vegetables, and fresh bread. She nibbled half-heartedly, her appetite dulled by the doubt clouding her mind. She finally set the food aside, and took her notes to bed with her.

She read for a while and when sleep claimed her, it was fitful and haunted by dreams of chilling mountain winds and jagged spears piercing Rhezan's thick scales.

THE NEXT SEVERAL days passed much the same. Each morning, Nyra rose early, dressed, and then ate breakfast. She visited the library, where she pored over other potential cures. Scribes brought her any volumes from their other archives that might hold relevant knowledge, though she found endless circles of repeated lore.

She made a point of speaking with the stewards responsible for procuring supplies. They consistently reported that disruptions along the trade routes from Desmir were growing worse. Carts were turned away at guarded passes. Local medicinal plants were meager substitutes for the stronger ones she required. In all this time, she did not see the king. He seemed to have disappeared as completely as his son.

Thomas continued to hover, quietly pointing out corners of the library she might have missed, leading her to lesser-known wings of the fortress that stored dusty bundles of scrolls. He rarely had good news about the prince's whereabouts. Rumors circulated among the staff. Some insisted Rhezan had flown out of the kingdom entirely, while others said he might be hiding in an abandoned watchtower to the north. None provided real comfort.

On the fourth day after Rhezan's departure, Nyra found her frustration mounting. She had begun to fear the time they'd lost when she could have been testing cures on him. Could the cursed prince simply vanish forever, lost to his own bitterness and the dangers of Sky Lances?

She returned to her chamber that evening, shoulders heavy with disappointment. Yet just as she settled onto a chair by the hearth, a steward knocked on her door. Startled, she set her notes aside and bid him enter.

He bowed his head with profound courtesy. "My lady, word has reached us that the guards at the gate reported a large, black-scaled creature swooping over the ramparts before disappearing into the deeper caverns beyond the castle. It seems the prince has returned home."

Relief hit her in a wave so sharp it stole her breath. "Thank you. Do we know if he is... well?"

The steward's gaze flicked down. "He did not appear injured. However, he seemed in no mood for conversation. Shall I convey a message on your behalf?"

Nyra sighed, standing quickly. She hated using emissaries to send messages; she much preferred fact-to-face conversations so misunderstanding were kept to a minimum. "Yes. Please let him know I would like to see him as soon as possible. He has been gone for days, and I..." She swallowed an upsurge of emotion. "We need to talk."

The steward bowed again. "I will pass along your request, my lady."

Once the steward left, Nyra sat on in a chair next to a bookcase and stared into the low-burning coals in the fireplace. Her thoughts were a jumbled mix of relief and nervous anticipation and absolute frustration over the time they had lost while Rhezan was gone. She had tried so hard to plan a method for lifting his curse, yet Rhezan was treating it with such casual disregard, as if the urgency belonged only to her, not to the man whose life still hung in the balance.

If he continued acting like a child, stomping his feet, and literally flying off in a rage, she'd have to figure out a way to defuse his temper. Perhaps his travels had relaxed him a little, and he would be more willing to talk after blowing off steam.

She spent the next few hours pacing. Memories of their brief, uneasy conversation in the Great Hall touched her thoughts. She recalled the flash of sorrow she had seen in his eyes on occasion. How quickly frustration reared whenever she pressed him too hard. Now that he was back, would he be even angrier, or might he be ready to let her help?

At last, Thomas arrived at her chamber door to deliver

the prince's reply. One look at his glum face made Nyra's heart tighten. He gave a tentative shrug. "I am sorry. The prince sent one of his own guards to pass word. The message is short."

Nyra's voice came out unsteady. "What did he say?"

Thomas released a slow breath. "Not yet. He's not ready to talk."

The words stung more than Nyra cared to admit. She pressed her lips together, struggling to hide her disappointment. Thomas lowered his gaze, apparently unable to offer further consolation. In the silence that followed, she exhaled and willed the sting in her eyes to fade.

"Thomas, I need a favor," she said. "Tell the king what's going on. He needs to have another talk with his son."

"He's already on his way down to the caverns, my lady," Thomas replied solemnly. "And he is not amused."

CHAPTER

EIGHT

Nyra shifted in her seat at one of the long tables in the Great Hall. She had chosen a spot halfway down, away from the door and the high dais. She always felt too exposed at either end. People still watched her with suspicious eyes. She talked to the others at court, on occasion, and even tried to make a friend or two among the women courtiers. She found them extremely polite and unfailingly detached. They seemed to be waiting for her to fail and be sent on her way.

The tall, flickering torches in the sconces cast warm light around the otherwise dim hall, causing Nyra's shadow to flicker on the stone floor along with them. Outside, the wind howled across the ramparts, reminding her that the mountain nights were never truly gentle. With the season turning colder, each evening felt like a warning of how harsh life in Varynth Hold could become.

There was an enormous meal waiting for her: roasted pheasant with a glaze of honey and herbs, thick slices of fresh bread still warm from the oven, and bowls of buttered root vegetables spiced just enough to make her mouth water. A pot of venison stew let off rich, savory steam beside a pitcher of mulled wine that smelled of clove and orange peel. Nearby, a soft cheese had been split open next to a dish of tart berry compote, and a tray of dried fruits and sugared nuts rounded out the feast. Everything shimmered in the candlelight, tempting and perfectly prepared.

She tried to be glad for the ample food, she certainly never ate like that at home, but found herself picking at the bread without real appetite. The fortress air seemed to sap her hunger, an unspoken tension crawling beneath her skin.

Her satchel rested on the bench beside her. Her time in the library hadn't been a complete waste, but she'd spent so much time researching and reading and taking notes that the words on the pages blurred before her eyes until she stopped in frustration. None of them contained the fresh insights she so desperately needed.

Shaking away those thoughts, she forced herself to retrieve her notes from her bag, hoping that reading her notes would somehow illuminate something she missed even though she'd read them dozens of times. Yet when she held the crinkling pages, she found no real motivation to read them. Her eyelids felt heavier than usual, and her head pounded with the ache of overwork.

The sound reached her first—distant but unmistakable. A deep, rhythmic thud reverberated through the stone floor, steady as a war drum. Between each heavy footfall came the scrape of talons against flagstone, sharp and deliberate, echoing down the corridor like the slow tolling of a bell. The torches along the walls flickered as a faint draft pushed ahead of him, stirring the air with the weight of something vast and ancient.

Slowly, she raised her gaze. Prince Rhezan padded into the Great Hall, claws clicking softly on the flagstone floor. He was in his smaller dragon form, his scaled head still tall enough to tower over her. His wings, draped along his sides, looking a little droopy, and Nyra immediately sensed his fatigue. She found herself wondering, not for the first time, how he managed this size at will. Could he become small enough to perch on a mantel or curl up in a pet's bed? The mental image of Rhezan the size of a cat, curling up next to the fire, almost made her smile. It was a marvel of magic and curse combined that he could shift his form with such fluidity, though it undoubtedly cost him strength.

He did not announce himself or offer greeting. Three servants, busy clearing the far end of the table, froze at the sight of him. They traded nervous looks, then bowed their heads and hurried off, leaving a faint hush in their wake. Only the snap of the hearth fire behind Nyra and the swirl of the wind outside broke the silence.

Rhezan walked toward the massive fireplace. His claws tapped the stones, each click echoing with an odd, hollow ring. When he reached the hearth, he let out a low rumble and lowered himself onto his haunches. The firelight gleamed across the elegant ridges of his obsidian scales, revealing faint veins of crimson along their edges. Nyra thought he looked worn, like someone who had not slept in days, though it was always difficult to decipher his expressions.

She cleared her throat softly and stood, sliding around the edge of the table until she was several paces behind him. The air near the fireplace held a comforting warmth, a gentle reprieve from the fortress chill that permeated even these grand halls. She set her gaze on the subtle drooping of his shoulders.

"Prince Rhezan," she said quietly.

His head half-turned, revealing one bright golden eye that shone more dimly than usual. He exhaled, and the warmth of his dragon breath stirred the logs in the hearth, sending embers dancing upward.

She took another step, stopping so that he would not feel crowded. "Are you all right? You look... tired."

Rhezan's tail curled in a slow arc across the polished floor. "I cannot sleep," he said. His voice in this scaled shape always carried a distant rumble. "I cannot eat, either. Just restlessness pounding in my veins."

Nyra glanced at the table where her untouched food sat. She wondered if offering him anything would help, but she suspected it would be pointless. Thomas had told her Rhezan's turbulent moods often killed any appetite he might have. Instead of pressing him about it, she asked, "Is there something I can do?"

He was silent for a few breaths. His gaze drifted from the fire to the floor and back again. Then he looked at her, uncertainty flickering in his eyes. "Reading helps me calm down sometimes," he said, voice hushed as if he disliked admitting this vulnerability. "I cannot read with these eyes as easily. My dragon sight is not very sharp for small letters."

Nyra's heart pinched with quiet empathy. She recognized what it cost him to confess his needs. She offered a small nod and moved toward the table, collecting her satchel of notes and the thin poetry book she had borrowed from the library's less restricted shelves. "I can read to you, if you like?"

His tail thumped once, a quick sign of tension. She almost thought he might lash out or dismiss her offer. Then he lowered his gaze. "Yes, please," he said, so quietly that she might have missed it over the crackle of the fire if not for how closely she watched him.

She came closer still, settling herself on a bench near the hearth so that Rhezan could hear her clearly. The flames cast shadows across his scales, a thousand faint reflections dancing around his draconic contours. She opened the slim volume and let her eyes roam over the lines, picking a piece she recalled for its vivid imagery of open fields and far-off shores.

Clearing her throat, she began to read. Her voice trembled with the first few lines, but she quickly steadied as she fell into the rhythm of the poem's meter. The words painted images of rolling green hills, waves lapping at a starlit beach, and the softness of summer breezes carrying the promise of home. She did her best to enunciate each phrase. Rhezan listened in silence, though his tail swayed slowly, as if the verses were reaching him in ways he struggled to show.

She turned the page. "Here, there is rest in the hush of morning dew," she read. "Beneath the wide, unbroken sky, hearts beat in quiet unity." The poem spun pictures of calm idyll, dreamlike and protected from conflict.

When she lifted her gaze briefly, she saw Rhezan's head tilted slightly as if lost in his thoughts. His eyelids were partly closed. She hoped to catch a glimpse of the man King Vorian had described: the one who once loved music and poetry, who found solace in the gentle side of existence. Though she concentrated hard on those images, she couldn't see the man he had been inside the monster he was now.

"I once went sailing with my father," he said. His voice was a deep, low rumble but still had a vulnerable quality to it. His tail flicked in a subdued motion. "We traveled to a distant port. I remember the water's endless horizon and how the salt air crept into every cabin and corridor. I lost myself in it. I used to think... that was freedom."

It was such a surprise to hear him talk that way, Nyra nearly gasped in astonishment. "What brought that memory up?"

"When I fly, I think of the times I've felt free as a human. Traveling, being on the ocean, always makes me feel free."

Nyra smiled softly, though a pinch of something wistful tugged at her chest. "That sounds... lovely," she said, folding her hands in her lap. "I've never seen the ocean. I've only seen drawings in books, and heard the stories traders tell when they pass through my village."

Rhezan's golden eyes remained on the fire. "When have you felt free?" he asked.

She hesitated, just long enough to feel the truth get stuck in her throat. The real answer was complicated. Her life was filled with long days treating the sick, expectations from people who never stopped needing something, and the weight of her blood-magic secrets she kept from almost everybody.

She thought about telling him but this night wasn't about her sad stories. Rhezan was trusting her with something rare and honest, and she wouldn't burden him in return.

"I felt free when I was a child," she said. "There was a field near our home that filled with wild daisies every spring and summer. My mother and I would walk there together, and I'd pick as many as I could carry. We'd weave crowns from them and pretend we were forest queens." She gave a soft, almost embarrassed laugh. "I don't think I've ever felt lighter than I did in those moments. No duties. No expectations. Just sun and wind and my hand in hers."

"You miss her very much."

A lump formed in her throat. Oh, how she wished she could talk to her mother now. She'd know how to talk Nyra through the impossible task of liberating a man from a dragon. "Yes. Very much." She felt the tears welling in her eyes but refused to let them fall. Rhezan was still staring into the fire, so she hoped he couldn't see how close she was to tears. She blinked rapidly to hold them back.

Nyra let the poetry book rest on her lap. She did not want to interrupt the conversation. She watched his expression, reading subtle changes in his posture. "You must have loved your mother very much, too," she murmured.

He nodded slowly, a stuttering motion that looked almost human. "I did. Now I cannot decide if I truly remember her or if she was just a dream." His claws tapped in a slow rhythm. A delicate screech punctuated every move. "Everything I used to be feels blurred. Anger just makes it worse."

Nyra's chest grew tight. She yearned to offer comfort but knew that too much sympathy could make him bristle. Instead, she continued reading the lines about open skies and tranquil waters, weaving the poem's gentle hush over the room. The crackling logs lulled them into a semblance of peace.

When she finished, the silence lingered. She closed the book, pressing it against her knees. "I can read more if you want," she offered softly. "Or we can talk about the witch who cursed you."

Rhezan made a startled grunting noise. "Wait," he said. "You know that story?"

The question caught her off guard. She remained still for a second. "Yes. I asked Jori and Harmond what happened and they told me," she admitted, choosing her words carefully. "They said a witch you were in love with felt spurned when your father demanded you break off the relationship because of who she was and she wasn't a noblewoman. That's why she put the dragon curse on you."

"I was not in love with her. She was the one who tricked me into bed and, like a fool, I didn't see her for who she was until too late."

She could hear the anguish in his voice. Nyra knew she must tread very carefully so she wouldn't set off Rhezan's temper again.

"Do you remember anything about the ritual she performed? The incantations she chanted, the herbs or potions she used. Anything would help me do what I need—"

He spun on her, wild and threatening. "Why did you even want to know any of that? So you can gossip?"

Nyra saw his scales ripple with tension. The deep rub of his tail across the stone floor conveyed stress. She set the poetry book aside on the bench. "No, of course not. I... well, I thought maybe understanding more about her rituals might help me find the keys to breaking the curse now."

His next breath emerged as a low, rumbling exhalation, punctuated by a flicker of heat that caused the embers in the fireplace to flare up. "They do not know the truth," he said coolly. "They cling to a version that places all blame on me and my father for hurting her, but it is more complicated than that. My father's advisors never heard what really happened. They only saw me change."

Nyra felt her heart pound. She wanted to ask further. But something in his tone warned her that she was treading on dangerous ground. "If you are ready to share, I will listen," she said, voice gentle.

His tail lashed suddenly, the movement abrupt enough to make Nyra catch her breath. She watched him grit his teeth—draconic fangs large enough to tear through oak. Whatever words he swallowed, they burned in his throat. "It is not so simple, Healer," he snapped, voice rising with a raw edge. "No, I do not want to talk about it. Every one of my father's privy councilors tells that same tired lie like it's a morality lesson about the dangers of trusting a witch, and I am the villain for bedding her."

Nyra's mouth opened, but Rhezan shook his head before she could speak. She was a witch, too, of course, but she had always called herself a healer, and she'd never used her magic to harm anyone. Still, if what Rhezan said was true, it made her wonder: did Harmond and Jori truly trust her, or were they simply following the king's orders, and holding their noses whenever she was around?

Rhezan's golden eyes flared with fresh anger, the earlier calm obliterated in a single heartbeat. "They do not care about me. They care only for the stability of the kingdom. The curse is what it is. And I'm the one suffering from it."

She forced herself to remain steady, though her pulse raced. "I am not anything like them," she said quietly. "I care about you, Rhezan."

He fixed her with a furious glare. For a moment, she thought he might turn his flames on the entire hall. The tension in his body rippled outward, raising the ridge of spines along his neck. A faint glow flickered inside his throat, and the air in front of her felt hotter. Her instincts screamed at her to back away, but she refused to flee. She had seen him like this before, struggling to contain pain behind anger.

"Stop prying into the past," he spat, tail lashing toward the hearth. Sparks flew where the tip of his tail struck the glowing logs, and a trembling hush fell over the Great Hall. "You think hearing one more retelling of how that witch tricked me and then cursed me will help matters? Do you not see she has cursed me to live centuries this way? A dragon's lifespan is infinitely longer than a human's. I will still be here when your great-great-great-grandchildren are nothing but dust."

Nyra rose slowly from the bench, her palms damp with persperation. She had made him revisit a wound that still bled, and he was pushing her away the only way he knew how. She took a shallow breath. "I never intended to pry. I promise. Just... let me help you find the truth we might need to save you."

He let out a roar that rattled everything in the room: the table behind her, the mugs, plates, and her meager supper clattering. The sound sent vibrations through Nyra's chest. He snapped his jaws shut, then spun in place, claws scraping stone as he stormed from the hearth toward the open corridor. The servants who had lingered beyond the pillars backed against the walls, eyes wide. Rhezan disregarded everyone, his tail slithering in furious arcs behind him.

He vanished through the wide doors a second later,

leaving a heavy hush. Only the wavering glow of the fire and the pounding in Nyra's ears remained. She stared at the path he had taken. Her body felt taut, adrenaline pulsing in her veins. Slowly, she pressed her palms to the front of her skirts, trying to quell an anxious tremor. She heard the distant echo of clawed steps fading deeper into Varynth Hold's corridors, likely heading for the subterranean cavern where he could assume his full dragon form in privacy.

The hall felt emptier than ever. Nyra's chest constricted as she replayed the fury in his eyes. She remembered the flicker of heartbreak beneath that anger, the hint of a man who still carried old betrayals close to his heart. She swallowed. Here, by the abandoned hearth, she was left with a swirl of guilt and worry.

CHAPTER

NINE

That night, in bed, Nyra was caught in a nightmare she could not escape. The cavern around her in that dream was dark, lit only by the incessant crack of lightning slicing through the sky. A robed figure moved near a wounded dragon, chanting in a voice that raised every hair on Nyra's body. The words were guttural, laced with power she recognized as something twisted at its core, as they reverberated against the cold stone walls.

Blood pooled on the stone floor. She could hear the dragon's low, ragged breathing, as if it was trapped between rage and terror. Each time the hooded figure's voice rose, a spark of lightning exploded overhead, illuminating the sickening scarlet that spread farther beneath the beast. Somehow, Nyra knew this was a ritual meant to corrupt, to bind the dragon's essence to something vile. She wanted to move, to intervene, but her limbs refused to obey. Her throat constricted with horror at the scene.

When the figure turned to face her, shadows hid its features. Only faint glimmers of light revealed the black sweep of cloth draped around its shoulders. Then the voice changed into a deep, echoing hiss. The dragon on the ground writhed, great claws scraping on slick rock, its anguished roar slicing through Nyra's thoughts.

Lightning flashed once more, so bright it consumed her entire field of vision, and she heard her name echo in the thunder. Nyra. Yet no one else stood beside her. She felt alone in that place, unmoored from anything familiar, drowning in the presence of ancient malice.

A final bolt of lightning thundered through the cavern, striking the dragon's flank. The blood on the stone lit with an eerie glow, as though the entire circle of fluid were a runic glyph. The pace of the chanting grew more urgent, each syllable pressing into Nyra's mind. She was suffocating on the magic that crackled in the air. She tried to scream, but the sound died in her throat. Then the robed figure jerked around, extending a hand toward her—

She jolted upright in bed, heart pounding so loud she expected the entire castle to hear it. Her bedchamber was pitch-dark, save for a burnt-down candle stub flickering weakly on the table. She gasped, trying to calm herself with a few slow breaths that barely helped. Sweat beaded along her hairline and dampened the thin shift clinging to her body. Her ears strained for any echo of chanting or thunder, but only silence greeted her.

Even so, the haunted sensation of that dream pressed in. She could almost taste the metallic tang of the blood she had seen, and a faint hum of magic shimmered along her arms. Her body felt as though it still hovered on that dividing line between the dream's terror and the real fortress around her.

She forced her lungs to draw another breath. The moment she closed her eyes to blink, the image of blood pooled around a dragon's scales seared across her vision. Shivering, she wrapped the blanket around her shoulders as best she could, and tried to will her pulse into a slower rhythm.

That was no ordinary nightmare, she thought. She sensed the wards in the fortress reacting, as though the dream had sent a ripple of energy throughout Varynth Hold. The air itself quivered with tension. Something in her blood-magic stirred, responding to the distant memory of power invoked in that dream. She pressed her hand to her sternum, feeling her own heartbeat thud dully against her palm.

"It was only a dream," she whispered, hoping that if she said it aloud, she would feel better. Yet her breath trembled with each syllable. She could not shake the feeling that she had witnessed a sliver of reality, perhaps a glimpse of the original curse inflicted on Prince Rhezan. She had read fragmented details about dragon transformation in the library books. No record mentioned a robed figure or a malicious chant quite like this. Still, the dream felt far too vivid to dismiss.

She swung her legs over the side of the bed and stood on wobbly knees. The floor was cold beneath her bare feet.

Her reflection glinted in the window's black glass—a pale face, hair clinging to the sweat on her forehead, eyes overset with worry.

Gingerly, she pulled her dressing gown over her night shift and paced the length of the chamber. She thought of how the stone walls sometimes seemed to pulse with magic. Tonight, it was not her trying to sense the wards. It was as if those wards were reaching out to her, resonating with the unsettled energy that threatened to take her over.

"Just calm down," she murmured to herself. She took a moment to breathe, inhaling the faint whiff of old candlewax and the slight chill of mountain air that leaked in through cracks in the windows. Slowly, the adrenaline in her system began to recede. She tucked a stray lock of hair behind her ear, trying to decide if she should attempt to sleep again or do something else to steady her frayed nerves.

The memory of the hooded figure and the dream kept her awake. She set the candle on a small corner table and stood near the window, looking out at the faint silhouettes of jagged peaks against an ink-black sky. For a moment, she simply watched the silent grandeur of the mountains. The nightmares in her mind warred with the solemn calm of the fortress walls. She reminded herself that day would eventually come, bringing the usual swirl of tasks and studying. She only needed to hold out a little while longer.

～

DEEP WITHIN HIS CAVERNOUS LAIR, Prince Rhezan woke from his own restless sleep. The stone beneath his scaled body was uncomfortably warm, though no fire blazed nearby. His claws flexed against the floor, memories of the dream stirring inside him. It always began with the faint echo of words that had once sealed his fate, but tonight there was more. He had seen a flicker of her robed silhouette, heard the hiss of her otherworldly chant. That voice congealed into the memory of the witch who cursed him, the scorn in her eyes, and the bitterness that had fueled her vengeance.

He inhaled sharply, forcing himself to remember he was in the present, not in the distant past. His body ached from tension and he knew he wasn't likely to fall back asleep. Fury burned at his core, but something else was there, too. It was subtle, like a faint heartbeat not his own, resonating through the fortress stone. He turned his large, scaled head toward the entrance of his cave, keenly aware that it was nowhere near morning, yet the wards carved into the stones around him hummed with a curious energy.

In a flash of recognition, he knew. It was her. Nyra. Somehow he could feel her energy, her presence, and it was a startling thing.

He had always been attuned to the energy in the fortress, had learned to sense the wards that bound the mountain's defenses. Lately, he picked up on fleeting signals that confused him, and it was only now that he realized the signals began the night Nyra arrived.

Tonight, the pulse he felt was stronger, as if her heartbeat lived in the rock itself. His wings shifted at his sides. It was not an unpleasant sensation, but it was troubling. He had never let another's magic, or spirit, reach him in this way before. He certainly had never experienced anything like that with Selivera.

Countless healers had sworn they could fix him. They had prattled on about herbs, incantations, even some who claimed that ancient relics could cleanse draconic corruption with a single wave of a wand. Each had failed. Each had left him more jaded, more certain he would never be free. Still, Nyra's resolve was beginning to convince him that she cared. She was different, and everything about her magic, especially that forbidden blood-magic, hinted at a power that might truly challenge his curse.

Yet nightmares existed for a reason, Rhezan reminded himself. Hope only made each failure more cutting. He leaned his head back and let out a low rumble, wishing the dream would vanish. Unfortunately, Selivera's face was burned into his memory. She was the robed figure from this new dream that blurred the lines between present fear and past betrayal. Rhezan wasn't sure whether she still lived, but the thought of confronting her and making her pay for what she had done to him was fodder for his more usual dreams.

Everything in him longed for flight in that moment. He wanted to burst from the cavern, climb into the sky, and let the cold wind scour away the gloom. The fortress walls felt too close, as though they tightened around him, echoing with the faint pulse of the wards, of Nyra's presence, of the dream he could not shake. He knew that leaving again would spark concern. The last time he had flown off, he had returned to admonishments and anxious questions from his father. He would certainly have something to say about his recklessness in exposing himself to the wider world. The alternative was to stay here, surrounded by the ghosts of a curse that refused to fade.

He let out another rumble, flaring his wings slightly, testing the tension in his limbs. He had the power to fly if he wished. Perhaps that was all he needed, for the night, at least: the knowledge that he could leave anytime he wanted.

He rose from the stone floor, each muscle bunching under dark scales. The cavern was dim, lit only by a single torch bracketed near the archway. His breath came out in a steady exhale, a faint glow shifting at the back of his throat. His mind strayed momentarily to Nyra. An odd pang twisted through him. He despised feeling drawn to someone who might betray him as so many had done, yet the memory of her reading poetry and the thought that her dedication and empathy were, indeed, steadfast, tugging at the hard shell he had built around himself.

Drawing a long, deep breath, Rhezan padded toward the cavern opening that led up through a sloping tunnel. Faint fires glowed in their sconces on the walls, but no guards lingered in the lower corridors at this hour. His footsteps could be heard, and felt, for hundreds of yards all around him, and he wondered if Nyra could hear the occasional talon scraping on stone as it rang throughout the passages. At a junction, he paused briefly to listen for the footsteps of watchmen, but there was only silence. The fortress slept, ignorant of the nightmares that chased him.

He passed the iron gate that had once been intended to contain him, though it had never truly done so. The first night he spent in his dragon form, he had ripped through it like it was paper. He had stopped short of tearing the gate completely off its hinges, leaving the ruined metal as a reminder to his father, and his privy council, that they could not imprison him.

He climbed the steps all the way to the top and emerged onto a ledge near one of Varynth Hold's higher galleries overlooking the fortress spires below. The sky spread above him, tinted with pale starlight and earliest hints of dawn. The chill air bit at his scales, an abrupt contrast to the stuffiness of the cavern.

He could see the fortress spires below, windows glimmering with faint torchlight. Somewhere in that mass of towers and hidden halls was Nyra, likely wide awake as well. A flicker of guilt stabbed him at the idea of leaving again without word. She had risked so much to treat his injuries, to gather the knowledge that might free him. A small part of him wanted to enter the fortress in his smaller dragon form, find her, and speak about these dreams that haunted them both. Yet his shameful need to protect his fragile emotional walls overwhelmed that notion. Better not to see her now, not when he still had bitter-tasting memories lodged in his soul.

With a powerful sweep of his wings, he leapt off the ledge. Cool mountain air rushed to greet him. The strain on his muscles felt invigorating as he worked them to gain altitude. Higher and higher he climbed, until Varynth Hold became only an outline against the steep mountain slope. His golden eyes searched the horizon for signs of open sky that he could vanish into until the nightmares lost their hold.

The fortress shrank behind him, leaving behind the lonely spires and the labyrinth of corridors. The wind hissed around his ears, and the half-moon cast a pale gleam across his scales. He breathed deeply, letting the cold mountain air fill his lungs, relishing a bittersweet freedom. Far below, the wards in the stone fortress might continue to shimmer, as though searching for him, but he refused to answer that silent call. He needed to outrun the robed phantom, the memories of failed healers, and the confusing pull of a woman who dared to use forbidden magic to save him.

For one beautiful moment, as he soared above the clouds, Rhezan felt the faintest stirring of hope. Maybe Nyra's presence was not a threat. Maybe it was the very thing he needed to face another try at transforming him back into a human. It was dangerous for his battered heart to hope, and he constantly waffled about what he wanted: take the risk and maybe become human or shut out the rest of the world and live the centuries that would spread out before him like an ashen blanket as a dragon. He glided past a jagged ridge, letting the crisp air wash away the immediacy of his thoughts.

Perhaps his dream was a warning for the future, or maybe it was just a fragment of his past lodged in his subconscious like broken glass. Either way, he wondered if this woman…this extraordinary, beautiful, headstrong woman…would keep her word and do everything in her power to free him. Whatever lurked in his dreams or dwelt in the echoes of the curse that held him, Rhazen hoped that Nyra intended to unravel it all the way to its ragged end.

TEN

Nyra traced her fingertips across the curly cript of the ancient tome, fighting weariness as she tried to keep her mind clear. Fourteen days had passed since she arrived at Varynth Hold, and every moment not spent sleeping or eating had gone toward researching Prince Rhezan's affliction. Around her, the library was brightly lit by a the candelabra overhead, and the candle stands around the table where she worked. She'd spent so much time there, the staff had begun to add more light so her eyes wouldn't get so strained. It was a lovely gesture and when she'd asked Thomas if he had anything to do with it, he simply smiled and said 'you're welcome.'

She had scattered half a dozen texts on the thick table: a grimoire of binding spells, an herbal compendium detailing rare plants, several parchment scrolls describing runic incantations, and her personal notes chronicling her own attempts to blend magic with healing.

She flipped one particular page, scanning rows of cramped handwriting that discussed conjuration circles. It proposed combining draconic runes with fresh water from a hidden spring, then layering the incantation with an offering of crushed herbs. Another book contradicted that method, claiming only a powerful potion brewed under starlight could break the hold of a shape-shifting curse. A third volume insisted any attempt would fail unless the victim's blood served as a conduit.

Absorbing so many conflicting ideas left her with a headache and no clear path. Still, she was refining potential solutions. She had jotted rough outlines on a scrap of parchment:

Ritual of Blended Runes: Carve specific glyphs into stone and empower them with healing potions.
Herbal Convergence: Use potent plants, powdered crystals, and an incantation at midnight in the presence of the cursed individual.
Blood-Infused Spellwork: Integrate blood-magic to amplify the fortress wards, forging a direct link to Prince Rhezan's draconic essence.

She had not entirely settled on one method, though a quiet part of her knew the final solution might combine several of those approaches. She closed her eyes and let out a soft sigh. While the fortress's library contained a wealth of knowledge, it also resembled a labyrinth of half-answers.

A gentle tap on the table beside her startled her out of her thoughts. She hadn't heard anyone approach but, to be fair, she had been engrossed in her work. She glanced up, heartbeat quickening. It was unusual for anyone to disturb her at this hour unless an urgent need arose. She set her quill aside and stood. When she answered, she found a breathless steward, eyes wide with alarm.

"Miss Nyra, the prince has been wounded," the steward said in an urgent voice.

"Oh, gods. What happened?" Nyra's eyes widened. As the steward continued talking, she was already on her way out of the library, running to her bedchamber to hastily gather what she needed.

"He went flying again," the steward replied as he ran down the corridor after her. "He came back with a wound to his left flank. They want you in the caverns immediately."

Once in her room, she grabbed her satchel and began to pack. Into the bag went her grimoire, along with carefully wrapped bundles of herbs: moonleaf, sunberry, and a potent dried mixture she had been preserving for emergencies. She added a pair of pre-made healing potions meant to clear inflammation, and a few small vials of salve that would prevent infection. Her thoughts raced as she threw on her cloak.

"Take me to him," she said. Her pulse hammered with dread. If Rhezan was badly injured, she wasn't sure she could test any transformation rituals until he was healed.

She followed the steward through the winding corridors, each step echoing on the cold stone. By the time they reached the entrance to Rhezan's cave, her breathing had turned shallow. The king and Jori, along with several guards, stood next to the prince, who lay motionless on the stone floor.

Prince Rhezan was in his smaller dragon form, though still larger than any human. She rushed to him and knelt beside his head, careful to keep her distance from his mouth in case pain or anger made him spit fire. She stroked the side of his snout.

"Is the pain bad?" she asked.

"Define 'bad'," he replied, his voice weak. "Sorry. I should have listened. Never should have gone flying today."

The king stroked the dragon's head. "We can talk about how you should be disciplined once you're healed, son."

Anyone who had ever heard a dragon laugh would never forget the sound. It's a rumble from deep within the chest, low and thunderous, like storm clouds rolling unhindered through an open valley. Rhazen laughed at his father and the sound echoed through the cave, rich and startling, edged with something primal. There was power in it, yes, but also a dry amusement that curled at the edges, like smoke from a smoldering fire. Nyra felt it vibrate through the floor beneath her, and despite herself, she smiled.

"My father, the jester," Rhezan replied, wheezing. "Thinks he can punish a dragon."

"You should get more than a stern talking to this

time," Nyra said, "but I have a feeling your injuries will do more to keep you out of the sky than your father's lectures"

Rhazen's obsidian scales had lost their usual sheen and something angry-looking spread across his left flank, forming ugly red welts that pulsed like they were alive. Jori stood a few steps away, conversing in a low voice with the king. They glanced at Nyra as they talked, relief and frustration mingled in their expressions.

Rhezan let out a low rumble, his eyes half-lidded in pain. Seeing him like that, an imposing, hulking creature reduced to ragged breaths, ignited a surge of protectiveness in her. She knelt by him, ignoring the way the rough stone bit into her knees.

"Tell me what happened and if you're hurt anywhere other than your left side," she said.

Rhezan grunted. "I flew over a village," he murmured. His usual rumbling voice sounded faint, each word labored. "I went lower than was wise, and they had a Sky Lance. The launched one at me and I dove straight down to avoid it, but it hit me anyway. I did not think a glancing blow would matter... but the pain became unbearable."

Nyra checked the wound, gently pressing near the raised welts. The very touch made his tail twitch in pain. The skin was hot against her fingertips, and an odd texture of blisters rose, bubble-like, along the edges. She placed a palm above it, channeling a tiny spark of her healing sense. What she felt made her skin crawl. "This is no ordinary injury," she said, glancing at the king and his councilors, then back at Rhazen. "It looks like you have a burn. Did they shoot a flaming lance at you?"

The king cleared his throat. "Sky lances are sometimes coated with wyvernbane, an old poison rumored to kill dragons. We never thought farmers and villagers would have access to a poison so deadly." He muttered a curse under his breath. "But it seems they do."

Nyra tensed. It made sense that farmers living under the fear of dragons would seek the strongest deterrent possible, especially if the rumors of impending war were true. "If the lance only grazed him, then the poison has spread very quickly." She examined the wound closely. "The blisters and swelling in his flank look worse than the actual puncture site." She gently nudged the blackened scale nearest the wound, grimacing at how the area was burned. "This is serious."

Rhezan's claws scraped the floor, an anxious rasp of nails on stone. "I feel fire racing in my veins," he admitted in a low voice. "My vision... it's blurry."

She nodded, forcing calm into her voice. "You need to stay still." She glanced at the steward closest to her. "Empty everything from my bag. I need the blue packet of ground herbs, one of the clear vials filled with the yellow oil, and the small bowl at the bottom of the bag."

He obeyed without hesitation and within a minute, Nyra had uncorked the vial of oil, poured it into the bowl, then mixed the herbs with it. She leaned toward Rhezan's wound. "I'll start with standard healing spells combined with these potions," she explained. "I have no idea if this amount is enough for a dragon but I have to start somewhere."

Rhezan's breath was slow and thready, and he seemed dazed. Nyra focused on her training. She poured a narrow line of the potion onto the wound. Immediately, steam rose where the mixture met the raw dragon flesh and scale. She channelled a quiet incantation under her breath, shaping the words for cleansing:

"By bond of flesh and healing grace, drive out poison from this place. Let Rhezan's life preserve its flame, undo the harm and mend his pain."

The mixture glowed faintly, but the brightness faded almost as soon as it began flickering. Rhezan clenched his jaw, stifling a roar. The welts remained, no reduction in their vicious color.

Nyra grit her teeth. She took a second vial, poured it onto the wound as well, and sprinkled a handful of ground sunberry leaves over the wound. She repeated the incantation, this time weaving in a small gesture of runic warding. Still, the poison's corruption clung to him, and the welts refused to subside.

The king's voice rumbled with frustration from behind her. "It's not working, is it?"

She shook her head. "Not enough." Stifling her rising anxiety, she remembered an older text she'd read: certain runes intensified the effect of healing. She sketched a few symbols across the stone floor with a piece of chalk from her satchel, and she chanted softly. Rhezan's tail jerked as a surge of discomfort rippled through him. The herbal poultice she applied to his wound gleamed brightly for a moment, then died back .

Nyra whispered, "Rhezan, can you hear me? How do you feel?"

He closed his eyes. "No different." His breathing had become ragged, each exhale heavier than the last.

She felt her stomach twist. Everything she had tried so far was failing to break through the poison's hold. She could sense the toxins deep below his scales, latching onto his living tissues, defying her usual spells. The memory of the repeated warnings about wyvernbane rose in her mind. The old stories said that only the strongest magic could counteract it... or perhaps a magic deemed forbidden.

Nyra swallowed. She glanced at her left palm, the one she had used in the past to draw out a single drop of her own blood. A wave of caution filled her. Blood-magic was outlawed; she had faced enough tension over it already. But if she did nothing now, Rhezan might die.

She squeezed her eyes shut, forced herself to speak aloud, her voice trembling with conviction. "I need to use stronger magic. I know you won't like it, but I think it's the only way to save him. I believe I can amplify my healing herbs and the runes by adding my blood—my magic—to them."

A startled hiss rose from Jori standing near the entrance. He looked on the verge of protest, but she lifted her chin and pressed on. "Wyvernbane is lethal. None of my typical salves or incantations are working. Blood-magic is the only chance he has."

Rhezan opened his golden eyes wider, faint sparks within them. For a breath, she thought she detected fear on his draconic features, but also something like hope. "Do it," he rasped, voice raw. "I trust you."

"Blood-magic is outlawed," Jori said through gritted teeth. "You cannot risk the king's heir with your—"

The king cut him off with a wave of his hand. "Do it," he told Nyra. "Do whatever it takes. I trust you, too."

Nyra dared not let that trust slip away. She reached for her small knife, ignoring the ominous quiet that settled over the cavern. She brushed her thumb against the blade, gauging its sharpness. Her heart pounded as she pressed the blade to her palm. The moment the steel pierced her skin, a bright jolt of pain shot up her arm. Warm blood trickled onto her fingertips.

"By the gods, this will be a disaster." Jori let out a bark of alarm. "You have to stop!" He looked ready to lunge forward but stopped, perhaps stunned by the determination blazing in Nyra's eyes and a cutting look from the king.

Nyra breathed through the sting, letting enough of her blood drip into the small mortar she had placed on the floor. Moving quickly, she grabbed a pinch of powdered windgrass and a sprig of dried moonleaf, then crushed them together with a pestle in the bowl containing her blood. The mixture turned into a ruddy paste as it mingled together.

Haltingly, she muttered, "Rot undone" under her breath to call up her own magical resonance, as she attempted to anchor herself to the fortress wards. She glanced at Rhezan, meeting his gaze. "Brace yourself," she said.

She smeared part of the thick paste across the worst portion of the open wound. The chalk runes she had scrawled glowed in response, flickers of red and gold rippling outward. Rhezan roared in pain, or perhaps surprise, as the paste sank into his injured flank. The color of the scales around the area pulsed like a heartbeat, as if feeding on her blood's power. Nyra felt something spark in her chest, a recognition that this was no small incantation. She held her hand over the runes, and let a few more drops of her blood fall on them as well.

A new warmth spread through the chamber. She sensed it flowing from her open palm into the lines of chalk, weaving in a pattern that touched Rhezan's scales. The hush of the cavern gave way to an electric hum. The red welts over Rhezan's flank began to quiver, almost as if they were about to burst.

Nyra's heartbeat thrummed in her ears. She felt the tension in Rhezan's body as if his heart beat in her chest, too. She saw how he tried not to thrash about in pain. A haze of steam curled up around the wound, and a low light shimmered around the edges of his obsidian scales.

In that moment, she felt connected to him more deeply than ever before. Her blood, his cursed form, the fortress wards all converged. She inhaled, fighting to keep the connection steady. She needed it to last long enough for the toxins to break down. The welts along Rhezan's side began to recede, shrinking ever so slightly. The scales lost some of the scorching red hue. Her eyes welled with tears of relief, though she dared not let her concentration slip.

Rhezan's chest rumbled, but less from pain now, more from the shock of feeling something healing him. Their eyes locked, and Nyra felt a strange stirring in her heart. She could only guess at what he felt in his own. The hum of energy traveled through her fingers, a mutual pulse that told her progress was real.

CHAPTER

ELEVEN

Nyra stared at Rhezan. He let out a shaky, rumbling moan. His breathing sounded steadier now, though exhaustion restricted every labored breath. Red blotches that, minutes ago, had bubbled as though alive were fading to a dull, mottled bruise. Relief flooded her chest, though a quiet dread lurked beneath that relief, reminding her that another confrontation about her blood-magic with the Harmond and Jori was about to erupt. But Rhezan was breathing, and he would heal. That was the most important thing.

Councilor Harmond, accompanied by several stewards and guards, ran into the cavern. He wore an intricately embroidered cloak that swished at his heels. He took one look at Nyra's bloodied hand and the luminescent lines across the floor, and his nostrils flared in anger.

"Is it true?" he shouted as he scrambled down the stone steps to the cavern floor. He was surprisingly agile for a politician who looked like he spent his days sitting in meetings. "Has blood-magic been used on the prince?"

Apparently, word traveled fast in the castle. Jori gave Harmond a forelorn look.

"This should have been stopped," Harmond hissed, turning on Jori. His voice echoed off the walls, sharp as flint. "Why did you allow her to continue this...vile practice?"

"He didn't allow it," the king replied. "I did."

There was stunned silence for nearly a minute, and Nyra watched as the king and his councilor looked ready to lock horns in a battle of wills. Of course, everyone knew who would win, but it didn't mean that Harmond wouldn't try his damnest to convince King Vorian that saving his son, at any price, would cost something he wasn't willing to pay.

"Your Majesty, we cannot allow this kind of magic to exist unchecked anywhere in the kingdom," Jori said, trying to keep his tone even.

It wouldn't do if he yelled at the king or tried to shame him into admitting that the leeway he allowed Nyra was wrong. That would be a good way for him to end up in the dungeon or have his head stuck on a pike as an example to others not to anger the king.

Harmond continued, "If we allow blood-magic in the heart of Varynth Hold, how can we enforce the law anywhere else? Do you grasp what chaos she might unleash upon us if she can't control her power?" He stabbed a furious finger at the half-glowing runes. "This fortress thrives on stable protections, yet here she is spilling her blood, threatening to unravel it all."

Anger sparked hot in Nyra's chest. "Wyvernbane poison does not respond to mundane healers' methods," she shot back. "If I hadn't acted quickly, Prince Rhezan would be dead now, and the king would be without an heir."

Harmond couldn't argue with that but he stared her down anyway. "No more of it. You can't risk the lives of everyone in this castle ever again. Blood-magic is unpredictable. One stray surge could warp the fortress's ancient runes or blow the fortress to bits."

She kept her tone steady, but her heart pounded so loudly she worried Rhezan would hear it. Her voice echoed against the cavern walls. "Everything about working with curses is a risk, Councilor. The prince suffered a lethal affliction, and I refused to stand by and watch him die."

Somewhere behind her, Rhezan let out a rough snort. Nyra cast a quick glance his way, noticing that his molten-gold eyes were no longer hazy with pain. The welts along his flank looked less inflamed. She felt a fragile sense of triumph, though she kept her composure. She could practically feel his gaze on her, but she dared not lose ground now.

Nyra glared at Harmond before turning to the king. She gently lifted her bloodstained palm up to him. "Are you truly committed to saving your son?" she demanded. "Because if so, I cannot be bound by the kingdom's rules that bind my hands when the prince's life hangs in the balance. Blood-magic is all we have left, and I will use it if it means reversing his curse."

She felt Rhezan shift behind her, scales scraping lightly over stone. The occasional hiss of his breath suggested relief from agony, though she sensed the exhaustion in him.

"Do not question my resolve to see my son restored." The king spoke directly to his councilors, who had the good sense to look sheepish. "Nyra has my full support to do anything required to make him a man again."

Nyra's pulse skipped a beat. She turned her head to see Rhezan shifting his massive body upright with painstaking effort. Steam rose from the receding welts across his flank, and the wound already looked less swollen. A faint glow still clung to the lines Nyra had drawn, though they flickered unsteadily as if waiting to see if they would be used again.

Rhezan spoke in a low, resonant tone. "I am glad we agree, Father. She saved my life." He glared at the privy councilors who now had the good sense to look scared shitless. "You have no right to stand here and threaten her for it."

He paused, taking a moment to steady his breath. Nyra's heart panged at the sight of his trembling forelegs, though he tried to hide his weakness. She could see the tension etched across the cords of muscle where scale met flesh. She felt his weariness in her bones, and as he squared his shoulders to stand up straighter, so did she.

Harmond swallowed hard. It was clear he was not accustomed to being challenged in such a way. Yet the king's command, backed by the crown prince's fire-breathing abilities, allowed him no easy way out. His Adam's apple bobbed as he tried to collect himself. "Your Majesty...Your Royal Highness," he began, "I only meant to—"

Rhezan's tail swished around, almost taking Jori and Harmond both out at the knees, but they jumped out of the way. The collision of scale against stone reverberated through the cavern as his tail hit the wall. "Do not question me about Nyra again," he said, voice like rolling thunder. "Am I clear?"

Nyra's cheeks heated at how fiercely Rhezan defended her. She had grown so accustomed to hostility in this fortress that a sudden ally, especially the cursed prince himself, sent a flicker of warmth coursing through her blood. She dared a glance at his face. Their eyes locked for a moment, and she saw a spark there, something that looked suspiciously like admiration. Her throat tightened. In that second, all the tension in the cavern melted into a swirl of gratitude and reverence. Her hand began to throb less painfully.

She returned her gaze to Harmond and Jori, who seemed uncertain whether to bow or run for their lives. After a tense moment, they both bowed and then they practically ran from the cavern.

She ignored the sticky dampness of blood on her palm. She turned to the king as Rhezan lay down again "He still needs a few days of rest," she told the king. "The poison's progression has been stopped, but he's still very weak."

"How long will he need?" the king asked. His eyes settled on Rhezan, and it looked like he might cry.

"Depends on how quickly he heals. A few days. A week, maybe." She pointed a finger at Rhezan. "No more recreational flying for you for a while."

Rhezan did not protest. He exhaled harshly, as though any grand show of defiance would cost energy he no longer had. "A few days...I'll be just fine," he said, and his gaze flickered briefly, a silent acknowledgment of gratitude.

A beat of complicated emotion passed between them. Nyra felt something stir, a tremor deeper than mere relief. She realized with a faint flutter in her stomach that, in defending her, he had trusted her more than he had trusted any other soul in Varynth Hold.

CHAPTER

TWELVE

Nyra paced the long aisle in the fortress library, her heart thudding as though it might echo against the shelves. This morning, after poring over more old grimoires with heavy, brittle pages, she had sent word to Rhezan, requesting he join her here.

When at last she heard the scrape of clawed feet on the stone floor, she turned toward the door. Rhezan emerged from a side door that led to one of the wider corridors, his still-healing flank hidden beneath sturdy linen wraps. He was in a smaller dragon shape this time, and she wondered if it was so he could conserve energy as he continued to heal from the poisoned lance. The scales on his side still bore marks of his wound, and they would one day make an impressive scar.

"Thank you for coming," Nyra said softly as she gestured him closer. She kept her tone gentle. He was enormous even in his diminished form, and part of her marvelled at how the library's high vaulted ceiling still might feel too low for him. "I thought you might be more comfortable in here than in the cold caverns," she said.

"No," he said in a joking tone, "you are more comfortable here. Typical human."

"Yes, I admit it. I'm the one more comfortable here, but it's easier to show you what I've found in these books here in the library than it is to carry them down to your cozy little cave."

"Fair enough," he chuckled. "You said you found something?"

"I did, and it might be important. Something that might change everything." She gestured to the large oak table behind her, where an ancient volume lay open to a page with overlapping runes and cryptic sketches of twining vines. "I sent a message to your father, too. I think he needs to see this as well."

She beckoned him closer. Slowly, mindful of his bulk, he stepped toward the table. The scent of parchment, old leather, and a crisp dryness filled the air. Although she should have been used to his draconic presence by now, the sight of him in the lamp-lit chamber brought her heart into her throat.

She steadied herself, inhaling as she laid a slender hand on the open tome. "While you were recovering, I kept looking for references to cure curses similar to yours," she explained. "Most texts only hinted at partial solutions. But this one mentions a specific ritual, called the Dragon's Ritual, that requires the use of a plant known as Emberleaf."

"But haven't you used Emberleaf already?" he asked. "When you healed me."

"No, those were other healing herbs. We're waiting on the MerChain traders to come through the valley. They're the best source of exotic plants and herbs we need for the ritual. The king has promised to buy out their entire supply if we need it."

She flipped to a page that showed a drawing of a spiky-leafed vine curling around an illustrated glyph. The vine was tinted faintly red, as though each leaf pulsed with hidden embers. "According to these notes, Emberleaf resonates uniquely with blood-magic. When used in the correct infusion, it amplifies healing incantations beyond their normal boundaries."

Rhezan arched his neck to look over the diagrams, his golden eyes brightening. He made a soft huffing noise. "And this plant can help me turn human again?" he asked, his gaze lingering on the page.

"I think it's a place for us to start." She traced one passage with her fingertip. The letters were small and cramped, faintly smudged with age. "Emberleaf is described as a living conductor between runes and the ancient and powerful magic not accessible through any other means than being an anchored in blood. When we combine it with the right incantation, it might just break your curse. Remember how I used my blood to clear out the poison?"

Rhezan nodded, a strange emotion flickering through his gaze. "I do," he said in a quiet rasp. "I have not forgotten."

Her cheeks warmed. "The right runes and incantation are the foundations of the ritual. My blood is the anchor. Emberleaf is the catalyst I think we need to connect everything together."

He lowered his head, the golden eyes narrowing as he scanned the passage. "Is that all?" he asked with a hint of wry cynicism. "A few leaves, a rune or two, some chanting, and your blood?" Despite the dry tone, there was cautious hope in his voice.

Nyra sighed. "It is not going to be simple. We have to get everything exactly right. Without Emberleaf, it appears my blood alone might destabilize the wards instead of fully catalyzing them. We have both seen how you're the privy councilors reacted to the blood-magic I already used. They will be furious if I use it on a larger scale. Even if the king has given his permission. We're must manage them as carefully as we manage the magic."

Rhezan exhaled, a low rumble rolling in his throat. "Your blood saved me once. I will not turn away from that power, no matter what they throw at us."

Those simple words meant more than she expected. She placed her hand on his leg, felt the dense, living warmth of him beneath layers of scale, smooth in some places, ridged in others. The muscle beneath was solid, coiled with restrained power, and she could feel the slow, steady thrum of his pulse, deep and unwavering. But there was something else, something she hadn't anticipated—a flicker of connection, as if her touch reached beyond skin and scale to the quiet center of him. It stirred a warmth in her chest that had nothing to do with magic and everything to do with him, and she wasn't sure if that terrified her... or made her want to move closer.

"I appreciate that," she replied. "This ritual is more complex than anything I have ever tried in my life. And it terrifies me."

Rhezan was quiet for a moment, his gaze steady on hers. Then, softly, he said, "I know you are. I see it in your eyes. You know what else I see? The fire inside that won't let you walk away from a challenge."

His head lowered further, until his snout was nearly level with her chest. "You face the impossible with shaking hands and still choose to try. If that isn't magic, Nyra, I don't know what is."

A pause, then a softer rumble. "Whatever happens in that ritual, I'd rather face it with you than survive it without you."

There were footsteps in the corridor outside the library. A moment later, King Vorian walked in accompanied by Harmond and Jori. The king's expression was solemn, though a faint warmth touched his eyes as he regarded his son. His privy councilors looked like they'd rather be anywhere else but standing in the same room as Nyra.

"Am I interrupting?" he asked.

Nyra bobbed into a curtsey. " Not at all, Your Majesty." She glanced at Harmond and Jori. Each wore an expression that hovered between wariness and barely concealed anger.

"We received your message about the Dragon's Ritual,

Nyra," the king said in a calm, carefully measured tone. "Would you care to explain precisely what it requires?"

Nyra took a moment to fortify herself. She was not sure how they would respond. She told them exactly what she'd explained to Rhezan, choosing her words carefully. Then she added the part she hadn't gotten to with Rhezan before the king and his men arrived.

"The wards in these walls are old and powerful, meant to protect the fortress from external threats. Emberleaf is a catalyst for binding magic together. Maybe I can find a way to use it in a spell that persuades the wards to work with me—to bind their energy to mine instead of pushing back. A kind of synergy, if you will. A bond between mortal spellwork and the lingering wyrm-magic woven into these walls. There are carved diagrams that describe a final infusion of ingredients that work with the incantation. I could be crazy, but...I think this is what's needed to complete that bond."

Rhezan shifted beside her, scales reflecting lamplight. His stance carried new tension at the arrival of the others, but he kept his voice level. "She speaks the truth. We have all seen the other mages and healers fail. If there is a path to end this curse, it likely hinges on more than standard healing spells or partial blood-rituals. Her discovery might be the solution that helps this ritual succeed."

For a moment, an uneasy silence settled around them. Then King Vorian nodded slowly, stepping nearer to the table. He studied the open page with furrowed brows. "Emberleaf," he said softly, testing the word. "I recall hearing it spoken of as legend in my youth. If it is indeed out in these mountains, I've not seen it. I am not even sure that the trade caravans would carry it."

Harmond sniffed imperiously. "We already know this herb does not grow on our mountain, my king. None of our kitchen foragers have ever come across it."

Nyra drew a steady breath and held up a book on local folklore like she was about to give him an object lesson. She knew what he'd said about having to wait for the MerChain Express caravans to come through the nearest village to buy the herb. But it didn't make sense to rule out the possibility it might already be right under their noses.

"I think you might be mistaken, Councilor Harmond. It's listed here in a book from the king's own library. If it does grow in the mountains, then we might have another source of it than just the traders."

She turned back to the king. "From everything I've read, I don't think we can afford to underestimate how much of this herb we might need. Without Emberleaf, I don't think I can fully attune to the castle's wards—at least not enough to heal Rhezan. My blood magic alone isn't enough, not with these wards. They're ancient, almost sentient. They don't just hold magic—they remember how it used to work. And they clearly don't like the way I'm casting now." She paused, focusing on the king. She understood that her words carried heavy implications for Varynth Hold's security. The castle fortress depended on its wards to remain strong. If her attempt to heal Rhezan misfired, the wards might be damaged.

She forced herself to hold his gaze. "Your Majesty, I do not want to endanger your castle or your kingdom. But you need to know, if we follow this ritual path, it might carry great risk to the castle. It is, however, the best route to breaking the dragon curse."

The king's gaze traveled between Nyra and Rhezan. She did not shy away from his scrutiny, though her stomach churned. After a moment, he released a measured exhale. "I made my intentions plain before," he said. "If it takes a forbidden practice to free Rhezan, I am prepared to grant the necessary allowance. The ward's integrity is of prime importance, yes, but so is my son's life, and the future of our kingdom. Without Rhezan, I do not have an heir, and that is as much a threat to our security as your ritual."

Jori frowned. "Assuming we do not wish to wait for the MerChain because it travels slowly, perhaps we should begin a search to see if Emberleaf still grows in our mountains. Any suggestions on where we even begin the search? The mountains are vast, and we do not have an entire army to spare just to hunt down a plant."

Nyra's voice wavered slightly as she answered. She looked at the king. "Since lifting Rhezan's curse is a matter of kingdom security, doesn't it make sense to put as many people on this search as possible? We don't need soldiers to find this herb, we just need willing people to help me look." she said. "Perhaps local guides know hidden valleys or caves where unusual flora might thrive. Or we can search old records from explorers who charted the region centuries ago. This fortress must have some archives with notes on where rare herbs have been found."

Harmond cleared his throat. "So we spend weeks or months rummaging through the crags for this plant? Meanwhile, the threat of our enemies looms large over us. Our supply lines are not secure, the realm is in danger we cannot ignore. Is it wise to send any of our people on a quest that might yield nothing?"

King Vorian's mouth tightened. He did not answer immediately. Instead, he turned to Nyra, as if inviting her to speak for herself. She squared her shoulders. "If we do not try, we condemn the prince to remain as he is. That situation will only invite more hostility from neighboring kingdoms who see an injured dragon as a weakness or a threat." She faltered slightly, feeling the press of so many watchful eyes, but she refused to retreat. "The risk is high, but so are the stakes."

Rhezan's tail flicked. "I prefer the risk of a search over the certainty of our enemies seizing every advantage. My condition has attracted enough opportunists. Another day wasted only strengthens them."

Nyra felt Rhezan's warmth through the space that separated them, a reminder of the fragile trust taking root between them. She noticed a hesitant acceptance in Jori's expression, though the wariness did not vanish. Harmond looked furious

King Vorian stepped around the table and placed a hand on the old tome. He studied the swirling runes, then looked at Jori and Harmond. "I charge you both as my privy councilors to do what it takes to find as much

Emberleaf as you can. Send scouts out into the mountains, send them to the MerChain caravans to ask their merchants if they have it, and to sell us as much as they can. I expect you both to bring me word of your progress." He turned to Nyra. "I expect the same of you, Mistress Nyra."

Nyra was glad the king had agreed so quickly to her plan. Of course, executing the plan would be another matter entirely.

"Yes, Your Majesty," she said, fighting to keep her voice even. "I will compile my notes at once. We will need to cross-reference older maps of the mountain that may indicate where the plants I need might be found. The seeds of Emberleaf are said to require intense arcane resonance, perhaps near lava tubes or fault lines in the mountains."

Rhezan gave another low throaty rumble, an echo that resembled tentative affirmation. "We have volcanic vents in the deeper ridges. Perhaps the area around those vents is a good place to start." He tensed, evidently recalling how these expeditions would unfold with him partially grounded from his recent injury. Yet the flicker in his eyes revealed a fragile hope. He was not giving up.

The king glanced toward his son, then at Nyra. His face softened as though some realization had struck him, something Nyra had already noticed: Rhezan no longer argued against her suggestions, and the quiet way her presence seemed to calm him, even in his wounded state, was unexpected. A subtle shift in King Vorian's expression made Nyra's pulse flutter. She suspected he saw the deepening thread of understanding between them, and that even if they would not name it, it was undeniably present.

"Nyra," he said, addressing her directly. "I see the resolve in you, and I see how Rhezan's anger is no longer an impenetrable wall. You have somehow done what no one else accomplished. I have faith in your ability to save my son and keep this kingdom intact."

His words, hushed in the vast library, filled Nyra with a heady mix of gratitude and fear. The two councilors stood by, listening. She could sense their reluctance, but they did not contradict the king's endorsement. Neither had any alternative idea for curing Rhezan. In that moment, King Vorian's statement was final.

Nyra lifted her chin, forcing a light smile even as nerves fluttered in her belly. "Thank you, Your Majesty," she said. "We will find the what we need and see this through. No pressure, right?" She tried to inject a note of humor into her tone, though her throat felt dry.

The king's faint smile revealed that he understood exactly how much pressure she felt. He gave a short nod, then turned to confer with one of the councilors, leaving Nyra and Rhezan by the table. Her gaze drifted back to the open text, its lines blurred momentarily by the rapid beat of her heart. She felt Rhezan's eyes on her, that golden intensity filling the air around them. The weight of responsibility settled across her shoulders, spreading all the way to her toes. She inhaled, letting the pressure anchor her, telling herself it was a reminder of what she must do.

She laid a hand on the book's page. As soon as they

had Emberleaf, she would attempt the greatest feat of healing magic she had ever dared to dream of. She whispered to herself that she was ready for whatever came next, no matter how treacherous. Then she closed the tome, feeling that quiet spark in her chest, the promise of a chance to free them both.

THIRTEEN

The next day, Nyra stood at the narrow archway that separated the courtyard of Varynth Hold from the harsh mountain wilds outside its walls. She pulled her cloak tight around her shoulders. Thin morning light bathed the craggy slopes in a grayish hue that banished any last illusions of warmth. Despite the crisp sting of the Drakareth air, she felt a flicker of relief each time she passed through the fortress gates. Being outdoors, even in the forbidding mountains, provided a small sense of freedom.

"Ready, my lady? I have our warning signals in case we need them," Thomas said. He patted the pouch hanging from his belt where he carried two signal flares in case of emergency. "I know His Majesty The King wants us to keep a close eye on you. Just don't give us any trouble and we'll have this task finished in no time. Probably."

Nyra offered him a tight smile. "I appreciate the warning. I promise not to wander off," she said. She glanced at the lonely peaks towering overhead. The bleakness of the mountains often rattled her, but now she found a certain comfort in their cool shadows. She was glad the king trusted her enough to let her join the search for the herbs that might help Prince Rhezan, and perhaps find that elusive Emberleaf to power the final healing ritual.

Thomas led her down a steep path that twisted around jagged boulders. The fortress loomed behind them, carved into the face of the mountain. Its dark stone walls glimmered in faint sunlight. Each precarious step brought them lower, deeper into the rocky valley. The route was familiar, a daily journey marked by stark beauty and a ceaseless wind that whistled over the cliffs.

"All right," Thomas said, halting near a small outcrop. "Where do you want to begin?" He took a moment to survey the ridge. "Plenty of shrubs. You sure they are what you need?"

Nyra breathed in, letting the cold air sharpen her senses. She knelt beside the nearest cluster of plants, examining slender waving blades that rattled in the wind. "This is windgrass," she explained, carefully harvesting a few stems. "I add it to certain poultices. It can calm fevers when combined with the other herbs. Unfortunately, it will not do much to challenge a draconic curse on its own."

Thomas crouched a short distance away, shivering in the cold. "That is what the king wants, right? Something to help fix the prince's condition. Heard it is serious."

She pressed her lips together. Rhezan's condition was beyond serious—he was cursed into a dragon's form, and only the slimmest hope remained that her knowledge might hold the key to setting him free. "Yes," she replied softly, "and I keep looking. I have not found any Emberleaf yet."

Thomas exhaled, stirring plumes of foggy breath in the thin air. "Well, if it is out there, you will find it," he said, surprising her with a moment of earnest support. "We still have a few trails left to try today."

Nyra clipped the last of the windgrass from the cluster, then stood. "Let's move on to that eastern slope," she suggested. "I saw a glimmer of silver leaves when we walked down, and it might be moonleaf."

A short climb brought them to a fracture in the rocky terrain, where frail stems with pale undersides grew in small clumps. Nyra knelt again, carefully lifting the leaves to confirm the crinkled shape that marked them as moonleaf. Her pulse lifted slightly. Moonleaf was not the miraculous Emberleaf, but it was still valuable and combined well in potions to help Rhezan maintain better energy during his convalescence.

She began gathering a handful, fingers growing numb from the cold. While she worked, Thomas squinted at the ridges looming overhead. "I never get used to these heights," he muttered. "That is a nasty drop." He gestured at a sheer cliff a short distance beyond their position.

"It keeps us all on our toes," Nyra said. She thought of Prince Rhezan perched high above these same slopes. Sometimes she glimpsed him on the terraces of Varynth Hold, dark as onyx against the pale sky. She sensed that he liked to watch the valley—perhaps scanning for threats or simply absorbing the space. The shape of his draconic body was more familiar to her now, and the idea of him surveying her movements from above offered an odd comfort she would not have admitted out loud. A part of her wondered if it was his way of safeguarding her hunts for herbs.

She finished collecting the moonleaf, tying it in a small bundle. Carefully, she tucked it into the satchel which was slung across her shoulder. Morning passed in this manner, quiet as she combed the rocky outcroppings with Thomas keeping watch. The day might have gone faster if they could speak freely, but Nyra found herself weighed down by her own thoughts. She kept scanning the crags for any sign of Emberleaf's distinctive red hue. Whenever she noticed a splash of color, her heart jolted with hope—only to sink when it turned out to be a stray wildflower or useless weed.

During one such check, she tripped backward over a loose stone and nearly lost her footing. Thomas lunged, catching her arm just in time. "Careful," he warned, helping her straighten.

Nyra's cheeks burned, though she tried covering her embarrassment with a quick nod of thanks. Scraping gravel from her pants, she stared at the bleak slope, frustration rising. "Sorry," she managed, voice subdued. "This place is not exactly welcoming."

Thomas shook his head. "No apology needed. Believe me, you are braver than I am for willingly scouring this terrain day after day."

She managed a small smile, chest tight. "Bravery or desperation, I cannot tell them apart anymore."

They pressed on. By noontime, the sun, though pale, offered a little reprieve from the chill. Thomas insisted they sit on a flat boulder to rest. He rummaged in his pack and offered Nyra a chunk of bread and a piece of cured meat. The gesture reminded her of the simple lunches she used to share back in her village, an existence that felt much further away than the mere weeks or months since she left. She sighed, recalling simpler days treating minor illnesses and never once worrying about royal curses or looming threats of war.

They ate mostly in silence. The wind hissed, making conversation difficult. Eventually, Nyra pulled her cloak closer. "We can check that eastern ridge before heading back," she decided. "If there is no Emberleaf, at least I can gather sunberry to stock our supplies."

Thomas nodded, so they began picking a route up the next jagged incline. The climb was steeper than expected, forcing them to use both hands to grip any stable surface. Twice, the guard paused to light a small signal torch. He did not release any flare, but the bright flame allowed them to find a halfway ledge. They scrambled onto the shelf of rock, hearts pounding.

"Do you see anything?" he asked, stamping his boots to restore feeling in his toes.

Nyra scanned the ledge. Thin patches of hardy brush clung to cracks in the stone, hints of resilient vegetation that thrived in the harsh heights. Her gaze flickered along the slopes until she spotted a cluster of plump, golden-tinged berries. They shone like tiny lanterns in the midday light.

"Sunberry," she said with renewed vigor. For a moment, her worries lifted. "That will help with overall stamina for Rhezan."

They stepped forward carefully, mindful of loose gravel. Nyra knelt, pulling off her gloves for better dexterity as she plucked the small orbs free. Each was more radiant up close, a shimmering blend of orange and yellow. She filled a pouch with them until only a few remained in the cluster. It was her habit never to strip the land entirely. Nature gave, but it could be depleted if one was too greedy.

Once the pouch was secured, she pushed a stray hair from her face. "I think that is all we will find today." There was a weariness in her voice she could not hide. That elusive Emberleaf seemed always out of reach.

Thomas glanced at the surrounding precipice. "At least it is not a wasted trip. We found moonleaf, wind-grass, and sunberry," he pointed out, as if trying to encourage her.

She nodded, but a pang tightened her chest. Every day, she returned to the fortress with arms full of lesser herbs, and every day, she failed to locate the one that mattered most. Emberleaf. Without it, her hopes of truly lifting Rhezan's curse felt like illusions. Still, she forced a polite smile at the guard's optimism. "We should get back before the sky darkens."

Thomas agreed, so they made the slow, careful descent to the main trail. The sun hung low by the time they returned through the fortress gates. Nyra's legs ached, and her cheeks were raw from the wind. Yet a sense of duty drove her to the library as soon as she could rest her feet. She would sort and label the herbs before nightfall.

Entering the library, she felt the hush envelop her. Shelves towered to the vaulted ceiling, laden with tomes and scrolls in every language. Cold lamplight bathed the long reading tables in flickers of gold. Here, the smell of parchment and leather replaced the frozen mountain air. She set aside her satchel, gently emptying the harvested plants on a spare cloth. She inspected each, sorting them by type. They would help Rhezan's health—just not retake the curse's fortress in his blood.

A quiet presence drifted behind her. She glanced up to see Prince Rhezan in his smaller draconic form. His obsidian scales gleamed, reflecting the faint lamplight. She realized her breathing had quickened at the sight of him. He remained an imposing figure, but as she saw him day after day, she began to notice subtle expressions in the tilt of his head or the way his golden eyes flickered with interest.

"Did you find anything?" he asked. His deep voice rumbled through the stillness, though there was something restrained in his tone.

She shook her head. "I brought back more windgrass and moonleaf. Found a fair share of sunberry too. Useful, but..." She trailed off, unwilling to highlight her disappointment. She glanced down at her work, hoping he would not press her about whether the foraging had been successful

He moved closer, claws scraping softly on the library's marble floor. "Every little step helps," he said. His gaze slid to the neat piles of herbs. "You do not need to be sorry."

Her fingers paused over the cloth. "I am not," she lied, voice catching. She was sorry for many things, though. Sorry he remained trapped between forms. Sorry she had yet to discover the solution beyond partial remedies that never truly set him free. She swallowed hard. "These can at least fortify your strength. You have been more fatigued than usual."

A faint twitch at the corner of his eye suggested he disliked mention of his weakness. "If it steadies me, I will take it," he rumbled. "Better than letting me wallow in these halls."

Their gazes met. Memories of the night they met filled Nyra's mind. They'd come a long way already, and still had further to go. She pressed her palm gently against the largest cluster of windgrass, sorting out stems. "Give me a moment to grind these," she managed. "I can brew something tonight."

He dipped his head in a stiff nod, then turned his attention to a broad oak table where a few books lay open. The library guard at the far corner bowed to Rhezan in silent acknowledgment and did not interrupt. Nyra resumed her work, pulse skittering in her chest. She tied the windgrass into small bundles for drying, then picked the sunberry from the cloth with a mortar and pestle at hand. Once the tools were laid out, she crushed a sample to test its potency. She smelled the faint citrusy tang. Satisfied, she prepared to stow the rest for later.

Rhezan remained close, scanning a tome. She could not help noticing that even in draconic form, he handled objects with deft care. He used a single claw to flip pages, mindful not to tear them. After a few minutes, his tail lashed softly against a chair leg, a sign of restlessness. She closed her satchel.

Their routine was set by now. Every evening she returned from foraging and worked in the library. He often lingered, especially since the king had given no new instructions other than urging him to remain patient. Patience, she thought, was never Rhezan's strong suit, yet the library offered a space they could share that wasn't a freezing stone cavern. She moved to sit in a wooden armchair across from him.

"Are you up for more reading tonight?" she asked. Her voice was quiet, uncertain whether his mood allowed for it. "I have a small volume of poetry that might interest you."

He turned slightly, molten gold eyes flicking toward the slender volume on the table. "Yes," he said in that subdued rumble. "Read."

She lifted the book, flipping through its pages until she found a gentle piece about a traveler lost in snowy highlands who found solace by a hidden spring. The lines were softly rhythmic, describing the hush of winter's breath and the subtle promise of renewal. Nyra read slowly, letting the verses sink into the quiet of the library. The words felt oddly fitting, capturing the sense of being hidden in a cold realm, waiting for warmth to break through.

She glanced up occasionally, gauging Rhezan's reaction. His head tilted, eyes half-lidded, posture less tense. He listened, though he said very little. When she paused, he would sometimes snort quietly, as if he was absorbing some memory or emotion the poem unearthed in his guarded mind.

The final lines spoke of hope—delicate, wavering hope that encouraged the traveler to keep moving, no matter how ruthless the cold became. When Nyra closed the book, her heart felt unsteady. She was not certain if those words were meant for her or for him or for both of them, but they lingered in every breath.

Rhezan blinked, as if rousing from a dream. "That was... pleasant," he said, his voice husky. The corner of his mouth lifted in what passed for a smile in his draconic shape. "It feels distant from this place, but I liked it."

The admission touched a quiet part of her. She set the poetry aside, meeting his gaze. "I am glad," she murmured. "Sometimes I wonder if these verses go unheard. You do not speak much about them."

He shifted his massive body, wings rustling. "I do not always have words," he said finally, "but they calm me."

Nyra's cheeks warmed, though she was not sure why. She cleared her throat. "Would you like to hear another?" she offered gently.

He lowered his head in a slight nod. "Yes. Please read me one about something warmer, if it exists."

A soft laugh escaped her, surprising in the hushed library. She opened the book again, flipping pages until she found a passage referencing the blossoming of sunlit fields. Her voice lowered, carrying the verses across the lamplit stillness. She read of orchard blossoms and golden meadows, of sweet breezes and gentle rains. As the lyrical lines wove images of a world far removed from these austere mountain halls, a hush settled around them that felt almost sacred.

In that hush, her mind wandered. She imagined Rhezan free of the scales, free of the raging curse, strolling through those sunwashed meadows as a man once more. Perhaps they would speak openly about all that had passed, about the lost years and the bitterness that had shaped him. The notion left her heart aching. She blinked hard, concentrating on the poem's last lines, finishing with as steady a voice as she could manage.

When she closed the book again, she saw the reflection of flame dancing in his golden eyes. There was something unspoken there. She let the silence linger, not wanting to force him to speak. At last, he inhaled.

"You asked me once," he began quietly, "whether I truly believed any magic could restore my human skin. I never answered."

Her throat tightened. "I recall," she whispered.

He exhaled, the sound like a soft growl. "I do not know," he said, "but hearing you read... it reminds me of how life was before all this. And it makes me want to believe." He fell silent, as if his admission had cost him more than he intended.

Nyra's pulse thrummed. She set the book down, clasping her hands in her lap. "I will keep searching for Emberleaf," she promised. "We are not done trying."

His gaze flickered toward her staple of newly gathered herbs. "Thank you," he replied quietly.

They lapsed into silence again, but this time a more companionable one. She watched him for a moment, noticing the slope of his wings, the faint tension in his forelegs. She sensed his yearning for something beyond these stones and spells—something simpler. She understood it better than she wished to admit. Perhaps they both longed for an ease that eluded them.

FOURTEEN

Nyra shivered the moment she stepped into the narrow corridor beneath the fortress. Every surface of this hidden passageway seemed to reverberate with an oppressive energy. It felt different from the other tunnels in Varynth Hold: colder, more foreboding, and oddly personal. She followed close behind Rhezan, who walked with a purposeful stride that made his obsidian scales catch the flickering torchlight. The gentle rustle of his wings promised restrained power, a reminder of the dragon that lurked under the stone arches. Though he had assumed a mid-sized form to navigate these claustro-phobic depths, he still towered over her, ever a haunting silhouette in the gloom.

Neither of them spoke at first. The air smelled of damp rock and hints of old ash, a mingled essence of magic and memories. A sensation of pressure, like a hand pressing lightly on her sternum, grew more pronounced the deeper they ventured. She recalled the wards woven into Varynth

Hold's foundations, how they sometimes resonated in her senses, but here that resonance was darker, as though the fortress itself recoiled at the path they traveled.

Eventually, the corridor opened into a round chamber with a vaulted ceiling. Thin veins of iron and obsidian crisscrossed the walls, capturing the faint glow of the torches Rhezan had lit along the way. Twisting runes decorated every inch of the stone. Some appeared fresh, their marks crisp and precise. Others were faint, older than she could guess, their edges blurred by time. Nyra drew a slow breath, forcing her heart to steady. She sensed something alive in those inscriptions, something that pulsed with the same dread that had weighed on her chest since they descended into these depths.

Rhezan paused at the threshold, his serpentine tail coiling protectively behind him. His golden eyes glimmered with a strange mixture of regret and resolve. "I have not shown this place to anyone in a very long time," he rumbled. His voice echoed off the stone, filling the chamber with resonance. "Not since my father tried to break the curse in those first desperate years."

Nyra stepped into the room. The runes swirling across the walls exuded a faint, sickly aura, as though each symbol still clung to the malevolence that forged it. The sense of being watched pricked along her neck. She set her hand on the battered satchel at her hip, seeking reassurance in the healing tools she carried.

"Is this...?" she began, her voice so quiet it felt swallowed by the chamber.

Rhezan nodded. "Where it happened. Where I was

first trapped in my dragon form. The magic that bound me is embedded in these walls. It stayed embedded in the rock, mingling with the magic cast by the first wyrm court at Varynth Hold hundreds of years ago."

He beckoned her closer to the largest set of runes. They wound in a jagged circle, carved deeper than the others. The groove seemed almost black, as if no light dared reside there. She braced herself and approached, kneeling to trace the shapes with her gaze. She recognized bits of older script—ancient Valendorian, replete with scythe-like hooks and elongated loops. Yet others were entirely alien to her, neither language nor sigil she had studied.

"I am trying to recall them precisely," Rhezan said. "When the curse took hold, I knew very little of the witch's craft. She used symbols that predate the libraries in this fortress." He lowered his head, breathing in the stale air. "I was never certain how much was the witch and how much was the magic already dwelling in this mountain."

Nyra swallowed softly, absorbing the tremor in his voice. She sensed how difficult it was for him to remember. "I can try to piece this together," she offered. She carefully withdrew a blank piece of parchment from her satchel. With practiced efficiency, she set a quill tip in her small ink pot and began sketching the runes.

Rhezan watched in silence. Each stroke she made was delicate and measured. She wanted precision—one missed curve might obscure the meaning behind these dark spells. As her quill scratched over the parchment, she felt that uneasy vibration in the back of her mind, a low hum scraping at her magical instincts.

She studied the rune, it's curves and patterns. It made her breath catch. Something in its shape reminded her of the wards that lined the fortress pillars, but twisted, like a reflection in dark water. She paused, pressing the quill's tip lightly against the parchment as a shiver traveled through her. The etched rock beneath her other hand all but pulsed with a hidden malice.

Rhezan noticed. "Are you alright?" His voice, low and rough, cut through the silence.

Nyra exhaled, nodding stiffly. "The magic is still alive," she managed. "It must have seeped into the stone. Even centuries cannot extinguish it. This place..." She let her words trail, not quite knowing how to articulate the sensation. It was as if the chamber itself resented her presence.

She resumed sketching, ignoring the clammy dread prickling at her spine. Rhezan stood protectively to her right, as though fending off ghosts only he could see. When she finished drafting the circle's perimeter, she closed the parchment. Her fingers relaxed around the quill, and she rubbed at the ache in her wrist.

"Anything stand out to you?" he asked.

"Many of these shapes relate to binding. Others are layered incantations. But there are a few I do not recognize at all." She tapped the folded parchment. "I suspect some part of this code might be undone if we decipher it fully. It could guide us to the correct method to sever your curse. If the inscriptions came from an older time—before wards were laid—maybe they have a flaw we can exploit."

Hope flickered across Rhezan's gaze. It was subtle,

evident mostly in the gentler tilt of his horns and the shift of his stance. "Let us hope so."

Nyra rose, tension in her legs from crouching so long. "I can analyze them again in better light. Maybe I will cross-reference them with the fortress library's older scrolls, or with anything that references the Drakareth region's earliest curses." She slid the parchment into her satchel and turned to face him. "Thank you for bringing me here. I know it is not easy for you."

He studied the runes one last time. His eyes gleamed with memories that hovered at the edge of his mind, too painful to speak aloud. Then, with a soft rumble, he pivoted away from the cursed wall. "You needed to see this, and to know the enormity of the challenge we face."

She pinned him with a look. "Yes, I'm quite aware. This is an almost impossible task but if we don't take a chance, then nothing will change. You'll remain a dragon. I'll probably go to jail. Our kingdom won't have an heir to the throne, and our enemies will overrun us." She smirked. "Did I get it all?"

Rhezan chuckled, a deep and vibrating sound. "You did. I always knew you were smart."

They left the chamber behind, winding back through corridors as silent as tombs. The oppressive hush weighed on them, relieved only when they reached a flight of steps leading upward. The stale air gave way to a sharpened chill. Nyra's breath felt freer, though her mind spun with the revelations etched in that dreadful stone.

At last, they emerged into a side hallway that opened

onto one of the fortress's broad galleries. A tapestry depicting dragons in flight hung over the carved arch, a swirl of faded reds and golds. Seeing that piece in the sudden torchlight made Nyra pause. The captured scene showed dragons soaring in a grand formation, free and proud. It reminded her that Rhezan himself yearned for that same freedom.

He caught her lingering stare and let out a tense breath. "What I would give to relive that life," he said quietly. "Unbound by this curse... a chance to take to the skies without feeling the sting of arcane bonds."

She touched his scaled forearm, a gentle, unspoken acknowledgment of all that had been stolen from him. "We will make it happen," she promised. "Somehow."

A faint tremor went through him, as though her words stirred both gratitude and fear. He started forward, leading her along the gallery's corridor and through a tall arched doorway. The corridor branched upward once more, then ended at a heavy wooden door that opened onto the fortress courtyard. Pale daylight greeted them, along with the crisp kiss of mountain wind.

Nyra blinked against the sudden brightness. The courtyard stretched wide, a sturdy stone railing at its far edge marking a steep drop into the valley below. Mosaic tiles underfoot bore the insignia of the Wyrm Court, though many details had worn away from years of sun and weather. She could see the stables off to one side, and beyond that, the gray expanse of the Drakareth slopes.

Rhezan drew in a deep lungful of mountain air, as if

shedding the last vestiges of the oppressive gloom they had left behind. When he turned to Nyra, his expression held a sudden brightness that made her heart jolt with surprise.

"Come on," he said, gesturing for her to follow him to the courtyard railing. "I cannot stay hidden in those tunnels any longer today. And there is something I want to share with you."

She went with him, curiosity tightening her chest. "What do you mean?" she asked, her voice still subdued by the weight of the runes she had just studied.

He laid a taloned hand on the stone railing, looking out over the valley. "During the worst of my transformations, flying was my only refuge. It was the one time I could forget the nightmare and feel... almost normal. But I have never taken anyone with me." A small, wry tilt curved at the corner of his mouth. "I suppose I never trusted anyone enough."

Nyra's gaze flicked to the valley stretching far below them. The mere thought of riding a dragon, even for a short distance, sent her pulse hammering. "You want me to fly with you?"

"That is precisely what I want." He turned, letting the mountain wind ripple over his scales. "All these secrets and runes... we need a moment outside of them. Will you trust me?"

Her mouth went dry. "But... how?" She gestured helplessly at his powerful draconic body and the unforgiving drop beyond the fortress walls. "I cannot just cling to your scales. I would fall off the first time you banked."

His grin widened, revealing a playfulness she had rarely seen. "My father once fashioned a special saddle for me. I suppose he hoped it would be used for ceremonial flights around the courtyard, to show me off to the realm. Things did not go as planned, obviously." He exhaled, but a lingering warmth stayed in his voice. "Still, the saddle remains. We can adjust it. The grooms can help. They will ensure the straps are secure."

Nyra stared at him, mind swirling with images of thrashing wind and dizzying heights. She had ventured over steep mountain paths, yes, but that was a far cry from leaping off a fortress wall on a dragon's back.

With a gentle shrug, Rhezan stepped away from the railing and waved to a cluster of stable hands who had noticed them. They hurried over, bowing their heads in polite acknowledgment of the prince. Nyra felt a flicker of amusement that no matter how many times the staff saw Rhezan in scaled form, they remained perpetually wary. Their eyes darted from his claws to his horns, though they showed no open fear.

"Fetch the black saddle from the storage room," Rhezan instructed one man. "The one we keep for... special occasions."

A stable hand nodded, disappearing around the court-yard's curved wall. Nyra found herself pressed into a swirl of restless movement: the rest of the staff gathered blan-kets and thick straps, while one older groom busied himself checking the buckles for wear or loose stitching. It all happened surprisingly quickly, as though this old cere-mony only needed a spark to be revived.

She took a small step back, her heart pattering in her chest. "Rhezan, are we certain about this? What if... I do not know... if you cannot handle a passenger?"

His eyes flared with gentle humor. "I have carried my father more than once. And in my smaller shape, I can manage you easily. Trust me. I promise no acrobatics today."

A solemn hush fell as two grooms approached with the saddle. It was larger than she expected, shaped to fit around the curvature of Rhezan's shoulders and ribcage. Rich dark leather had been carefully stitched with the crest of the Wyrm Court, and the edges were scuffed from prior use. The design featured wide straps that looped beneath his chest, plus a harness for the rider that included small loops for feet, ensuring a more stable seat.

Rhezan crouched in the center of the courtyard, letting the grooms maneuver around him. One fumbled with the straps, while the other arranged a layered pad against his obsidian scales to keep the leather from chafing. Nyra hovered at a safe distance, chewing her lip as she watched them work. Despite her racing nerves, she could not deny the strange excitement building in her gut.

She heard Rhezan inhale and exhale, centering himself as the pieces were buckledl into place. After a few tense minutes, the main groom stood back, wiping sweat from his brow. "Ready, m'lord," he said, stepping away from Rhezan's flanks.

Rhezan shifted, testing the straps that wrapped around him. The entire assembly barely shifted, locked into place with a series of buckles. "Nyra," he said softly, glancing at her, "come here."

She swallowed, stepping forward. One of the men offered her a smaller belt-like harness that would attach to parts of the main saddle. She gingerly slipped it around her waist and over her shoulders. Her heart thumped so loudly she was certain everyone could hear it. The older groom helped, guiding her foot into a small stirrup, then boosting her up until she settled onto the saddle. The fit was snug, enough to assure that she would not slide off if Rhezan took a steep turn.

Her fingers trembled on the front grip. She looked down at Rhezan's scaled neck, the faint ridges along his spine. He was warm beneath her, not the cold monster court gossips made him out to be. She felt his breathing, slow and steady, as though to calm her. Over the last weeks, they had found an alliance built on cautious trust. Now that trust expanded into something deeper, an unspoken promise that he would keep her safe.

"Hold on," Rhezan advised gently. "Relax if you can. I will start slowly."

Nyra squeezed the grips, legs pressing lightly against his sides. Her stomach threatened to leap into her throat, but she forced herself to breathe. The staff around them backed away, clearing space in the courtyard. In front of her. Rhezan spread his wings, the membranes glimmering with faint red undertones where the sunlight caught them.

She closed her eyes a moment, remembering the runes etched in that cursed chamber, remembering the vow she made to help him break those chains. Perhaps this flight was a glimpse of what he might become if freed. Maybe it was also a promise that they were capable of more than fear and regret.

Rhezan braced his legs. He opened his wings fully, the courtyard wind catching his scales in a sweeping rustle. Then, with a sudden surge of power that made Nyra's breath hitch, he launched himself upward. The courtyard fell away beneath them, the flight abrupt but graceful as he ascended into the open air.

Nyra's heart lurched. She clutched the saddle's handle, eyes wide, an exhilarated cry catching in her throat. The wind buffeted her face, carrying the crisp scent of alpine ridges and faint pine. The sensation of weightlessness stole her breath, but the harness kept her firmly on Rhezan's back. He banked once, gently, letting her adjust to the altitude.

She gasped again, this time in pure wonder. The fortress spires below looked smaller, the carved ramparts merging into the gray stone. A swirl of clouds hovered near one mountaintop, shining pale in the midday light. She had seen the Drakareth peaks from the ground countless times, but never from above, never with such clarity. It was terrifying and beautiful, an untamed world spread out beneath them.

As they soared higher, Nyra felt her fears melt into a strange delight. She loosened her white-knuckle grip, letting her pulse settle into the rhythm of Rhezan's flight. His wings beat with steady power, each stroke pushing them farther from the courtyard. The harness pressed snugly around her chest, but she could breathe, finally, and that breath brought a rush of astonishment at what they were doing.

She dared to peek over one side, glimpsing the fortress far below. Giddy laughter bubbled from her lips, part joy and part disbelief that she, a village healer who had once feared even the sharpness of a draconic roar, was now riding with a prince-turned-dragon across the open sky. Beneath her, Rhezan let out a low rumble, almost like a pleased chuckle. She caught the edge of his reflection in the sunlight and realized he was smiling in his own way, triumphant in sharing this moment with her.

The terror that had knotted her chest moments before was replaced by a liberating thrill. The wind tore at her hair and stung her cheeks, but she welcomed it, tears gathering at the corners of her eyes from sheer exhilaration. Everything below fell away. The heavy gloom of curses and runes, the political tensions coiled inside the fortress, the dread that dogged her footsteps—none of it existed in this instant. Only the sky, the beating wings, and the two of them breaking free of gravity.

Anchored safely by the saddle's embrace, Nyra surrendered to that feeling. It eclipsed the echoes of the darkness they had left behind in that cursed chamber, offering instead a glimpse of hope. Each rise and glide drew her and Rhezan closer, a shared, unspoken faith that perhaps, together, they could transcend the curse that bound them both.

In that heartbeat of soaring freedom, the fortress below might as well have belonged to another lifetime.

She leaned forward and felt Rhezan's answering warmth, the thunder of his pulse through the scales beneath her. A gentle current of air lifted them higher, and her fluttering heart quickened with each shift of the wind.

They flew on and as they ascended in a slow arc, Nyra's excitement only grew, each heartbeat a reminder that neither of them was alone.

FIFTEEN

Nyra sat at one of the library's heavy oak tables with her notes spread across the polished surface. She ran her fingertip along a vine motif carved into the table's edge and tried to settle her restless mind. For days, she had pored over volumes that detailed curses, wards, and the tenuous bridge between mortal blood and draconic power. Yet nothing felt like it could unify all the necessary elements. Everything rested on a precarious hill of half-seen solutions.

Rhezan reclined across from her, coiled in his smaller dragon shape so that his wings and tail might fit comfortably within the high-arched bookcases. His scaled flank gleamed in the glow of the library's lamps. The space hummed with the faint scratch of Nyra's quill as she made more notes about possible rituals. Once in a while, she glanced at Rhezan. Though his expression remained neutral, she sensed his frustration. The last few weeks had seen countless attempts to wrest meaning from cryptic incantations and archaic runes, yet they still lacked a sure path forward.

She spoke softly, partly to keep her voice from echoing between the towering shelves. "These references suggest we concentrate the wards' energy in the same place the curse was cast. It makes sense. The magic that bound you still resonates in that chamber."

Rhezan's molten-gold eyes narrowed. "The same cursed place that has haunted me for years. Are you certain it can help?"

"I can't be certain," she admitted, setting down her quill. "But the structure of these spells keeps pointing there. We might be able to harness the fortress wards more effectively if we align them with the original runic site."

Silence stretched. A faint drip of wax from a nearby sconce punctuated the hush. Then a distant knock sounded at the library's double doors. Nyra and Rhezan both turned as a steward in neat livery opened the door wide enough for King Vorian to stride inside. The king's expression blended relief and anxiety the moment he caught sight of them.

"My son," he said, greeting Rhezan with a soft incline of his head. Then he turned to Nyra. "I hope I'm not interrupting a crucial discovery?"

Nyra stood and smoothed her skirts, noticing how Rhezan shifted his wings in a guarded posture. The king looked more haggard than usual, faint circles under his eyes, lines bracketing his mouth.

"You aren't interrupting," Nyra replied carefully. "We're still sorting the best approach."

Rhezan lowered his head in a restrained bow to his father. King Vorian stepped closer, and his gaze flicked worriedly over the notes on the table. He lifted one scrap of parchment, scanning the lines of archaic script Nyra had copied. His voice took on a weary softness.

"How fares our progress on lifting this terrible curse?" the king asked as he placed the parchment back. "You have both worked tirelessly, but I must know: do you see a clear path?"

Nyra twisted her fingers together. She hated giving him incomplete news. "It's going slowly, Your Majesty," she admitted. "We keep finding partial rituals, half-formed theories, or spells that require more ingredients than the fortress can supply. We also believe the next attempt must happen in the cave where the curse was cast. Nothing else will align the wards properly with the runic magic in Rhezan's blood."

The king gave an acknowledging nod. "Then I trust you to begin preparations. But you must pick up the pace."

Rhezan's tail gave a slow, tense flick at that, but he remained silent. Nyra could hardly blame him. She, too, felt the pressure squeezing like a vise on her lungs. The king let out a long breath, then held up a small rolled parchment sealed in dark wax.

"A falcon arrived this morning," he said. "Carrying a coded message from Ambassador Sera in Telandria. I requested her presence weeks ago, and it seems she will arrive sooner than expected."

Nyra watched Rhezan jerk upright, wings twitching like a startled bird. His reaction caught her attention. She glanced between father and son. The king's mouth tightened at the corners as he continued, addressing them both:

"In her letter, Sera mentions disturbing rumors. Our neighbors to the east believe the Dragon Prince lies gravely injured after being shot down from the sky. They think the kingdom has lost its strongest defender. Which means they are more likely to plan an invasion."

A swirl of tension flooded the library in the wake of his words. Nyra's pulse thrummed uncomfortably. They had heard chatter about enemies across the mountains, but the knowledge that outside realms were poised to strike hammered reality home. Glancing at Rhezan, she saw how his golden eyes lost some of their usual brilliance. He dipped his head low, a shadow crossing his scaled features.

"They want war?" Rhezan asked, voice tight.

The king nodded. "Or at least a chance to exploit our perceived weakness. If they think you are dying, losing blood day by day from your wound, they will see us as vulnerable."

Nyra felt a flurry of conflicting emotions. She recalled how Rhezan had once been grazed by a poisoned Sky Lance, forcing her to use her forbidden blood-magic. Though he recovered physically, rumors must have spread. With the siege weapons out there, any rumor could stir an entire realm's aggression.

Rhezan bristled, teeth bared at the mention of war. "I

can fly over Desmir or whichever realm challenges us most. My presence would prove I am not dead." He rose slightly, a ripple passing along his obsidian wings.

The king's stern expression hardened. "No. You were grazed once, and it nearly killed you. I will not lose you to a direct assault from some fool with a well-poisoned bolt. You may not like it, but until further notice, you are grounded."

Silence fell for a tense moment. Nyra could almost hear Rhezan's heartbeat pounding in frustration. Even from a few steps away, she sensed how caging him touched an old nerve. Part of him still clung to the freedom of flight, that final escape from the curse's misery. Now it was being denied again.

"You think hiding me in these halls will stop them?" Rhezan muttered. His claws scraped the library floor in an agitated twitch. "Soldiers bested me once with a single shot. If they truly plan to attack, we should show force rather than cower behind walls."

The king held Rhezan's gaze, unwavering. "We cannot afford to lose you, whether or not the stories of your injuries are overblown. They will test our defenses soon enough. But I need to know you are safe—and I need Nyra to break this curse. The kingdom's fate rests on it."

Nyra swallowed. "I will do my utmost, Your Majesty. But the ritual is exceedingly complex. Blood-magic can only amplify so much. We require synergy with the fortress wards, and that synergy is strongest in the original location. It may take days or weeks to prepare runes and gather every component. We are not—"

"You must move faster," the king cut in gently, though his voice carried finality. "Time is not our ally. The realm depends on Rhezan's cure, and I will use any means to see that happen."

His gaze darted from Rhezan's fierce eyes to Nyra's anxious face: a father desperate for results. That paternal weight lay heavy in the lines of his countenance.

"Ambassador Sera's arrival will signal to others that we are not so vulnerable," the king said, forcing a tired smile. "But also, she brings her own diplomatic ties. I hope it may buy us time." He gave a short half-bow to both, then squared his shoulders. "I must address the council. Continue your work. I will await progress."

With that, King Vorian strode out of the library, the steward shutting the doors behind him. Nyra exhaled, shoulders dropping as the tension of the meeting leaked away. A wave of quiet pressed around them, broken only by the shifting of pages on the table. Outside the tall stained-glass windows, the sky was gray with approaching dusk, painting the library in a somber tone.

She looked at Rhezan, uncertain if speaking would calm him or inflame him further. He lowered his head, letting out a low hiss of frustration.

"So I am caged." His voice rumbled with bitterness. "Grounded, as if my father can demand the wind itself to stop blowing. It is humiliating."

Nyra edged closer. She laid a tentative hand near his foreleg, not quite touching him but close enough to offer comfort. "He fears for your life. I... might share that worry. The day you were wounded was—" She paused, remembering the horrifying sight of his blistered scales. "We do not want to see you in such pain again."

Rhezan's eyes flared, then softened. "I know. But I hate feeling powerless." He let out a long breath, tension easing from his rigid stance. "Still, I also see his point. If they shot me down a second time, it would break more than just my bones." He gave a short shrug. "People want to believe I can protect them from an invasion. A dead dragon prince would confirm the realm's collapse."

"No one is letting you die," Nyra said firmly. "We will find a cure. Then you can protect your kingdom in human form, or in whichever form you choose. But we do need the correct environment for the ritual."

That statement drew him back to the conversation they had before the king's interruption. "The cursed cave," Rhezan said quietly. "When do you want to begin your inscriptions?"

"As soon as I can gather the final runes," she answered. "The spells I discovered mention layering runes around the perimeter, then channeling power from the fortress wards. We would also integrate your own unique energies. We will pour everything into the exact spot the curse was first invoked."

Rhezan studied her carefully. "That is dangerous. If anything goes wrong... the cave might lash out or awaken some twisted echo of the curse."

Nyra tried to keep her voice steady. "If we do nothing, war will break out anyway. My mother always taught me that sometimes you must confront a sickness at its root."

That admission surprised her. She hadn't spoken her

mother's words aloud in ages. But if she had learned nothing else from her mother's old instructions, it was that ignoring an illness only allowed it to fester. Rhezan dipped his head in understanding, seemingly accepting her logic.

She brushed aside a stray note, trying to avoid letting her own anxiety show. "I think we have an outline of a plan. We need the right incantations, the Emberleaf to act as the binding ingredient in the spell to gain the wards' cooperation... and plenty of time to set up safely. But yes, the cave is certainly key to this ritual, too."

They lapsed into a momentary lull. Through the windows, the first hint of twilight glimmered on the horizon. She drew in a steadying breath. A fresh question nipped at the back of her mind. She recalled Rhezan's sudden tension when the king mentioned Ambassador Sera. It nagged at her, stirring curiosity.

She looked up. He had shifted to place his forelegs neatly in front of him, gold eyes half-lidded as though lost in thought. Seeking an opening, she inhaled and asked as gently as she could, "Rhezan... if you don't mind me prying, you seemed startled when your father said Sera is returning."

A flicker of discomfort passed over his features. "You noticed."

She nodded. "Yes. And I'm worried. Is there something about this ambassador that troubles you?"

At first, he did not answer. A flick of the tail, a faint clench in his jaw. Then, at last, he shifted his gaze to meet hers. "We have history," Rhezan said quietly. "We were...

set to marry, in a manner of speaking, when I was younger. But something came between us. My curse destroyed our official engagement, or perhaps her devotion to me. She left with my father's approval. She studied abroad and built a new life as a diplomat."

Nyra's heartbeat raced, though she tried not to betray emotion. She had wondered if Rhezan's bitter edges might spring from older wounds of the heart.

He continued, his voice low and resigned. "After the witch cursed me, Sera was a comfort. At least, at first. We rediscovered our feelings for each other and it, was a life-line for me as the mages and healers tried again and again to make me human again." He sounded like he might weep right then and there, but somehow kept himself together. "When it became clear that nobody could help me, and I was doomed to remain a dragon, Sera rejected me. She could not love...a monster. My father sent her away to Telandria to be our ambassador to that kingdom. Whether he did so to truly serve the kingdom or to protect her from me, I never asked. All I know is that she vanished, leaving me to figure out this curse alone."

Nyra felt her breath catch just slightly, but enough to sting. Not because of a distant past he shared with Sera, but because of the pain it still clearly caused him. His voice carried the hollow echo of abandonment, of a wound that had never truly closed. She had known he was alone for a long time. And it pained her

She looked down at her hands, still resting in her lap, fingers trembling slightly. Sera had claimed to love him, and then turned away when it mattered most. When he had needed her not as a prince or a potential husband, but simply as someone who wouldn't flinch at his suffering.

The ache in Nyra's chest sharpened into something darker. She had no right to jealousy. That wasn't what this was. It was grief—for the years he had spent with no one. For the echo of hope shattered by someone who should have stayed. And beneath that grief, a burn began to spread through her ribcage.

Sera hadn't just left. She had abandoned a man in agony and then built a new life as a diplomat, and, by all accounts, a successful one at that. Nyra could already see her—poised, polished, accomplished—returning now, walking these halls like she hadn't once chosen comfort over courage.

Nyra clenched her jaw. She would not let that woman hurt him again. Not while he still bore the scars of her silence. Not while Nyra was here, pouring her own lifeblood into spells, rituals, and impossible hopes for a future he might not even believe in yet.

Some kind-hearted beings might forgive betrayal if offered the right apology and restitution. But a healer? A healer remembers every wound—and she had just discovered one she intended to protect, no matter what it cost.

CHAPTER

SIXTEEN

Several days later, Nyra went into the Great Hall, balancing an armful of scrolls in her arms. She paused at the threshold to gather her composure. The lofty chamber stretched before her, illuminated by wide braziers that bathed the rows of carved pillars in a warm glow. In the center, Rhezan waited near the main hearth, his obsidian body coiled in a shape smaller than his fully expanded dragon form. The dark scales along his flanks caught the firelight, giving him a faint metallic sheen. His tail curled loosely on the polished floor, as though trying to appear more at ease than he felt.

She cleared her throat, and her voice came out calmer than she expected. "These are the fragments I told you about. They might shed insight on wyrm-binding and unbinding spells."

Rhezan rasped out a low rumble in acknowledgment. His eyes, molten gold tinged with flickers of crimson, tracked her every step until she stopped beside him. Despite the blazing hearth, the Hall still felt cold. She sensed his tension immediately, a guarded note in the way he held his wings pressed to his sides. Yet beneath that guarded exterior, she detected the same restless hope she carried in her own heart.

With care, she set her collection on a nearby trestle table, then pulled out a stool so she could spread the scrolls without scattering them across the floor. Most were centuries old, some written in archaic scripts she had only started to decipher. Several were grayed from neglect and others were crisp with faint burn marks, as if they had once come too close to a candle's flame.

Rhezan reached out with his foreleg, tucking his claws near the table's edge to avoid damaging the fragile parchments. "You are certain these references discuss curses like mine?"

"Certain? Not entirely," she admitted. She carefully unrolled a scroll, flattening the edges with her palms. "But many of the runes here resemble those we saw in your cursed chamber. Note the sweeping hooks along the lines. Ancient scribes called them vex-runes, named for how difficult they are to interpret. We found similar markings on the walls below."

Rhezan leaned closer, so close that Nyra felt the warmth of his body envelop her. His breath, slightly acrid from the power within him, mingled with the sweet tang of burning pine from the hearth. She pointed to a symbol shaped like a spiraled claw. "That one, for instance, appears in older Drakareth lore. It relates to binding a dragon's natural essence to the mountain stone itself. If so, we need a corresponding unbinding mark to free you."

Rhezan tilted his broad head, his horns dipping. "Show me what you have deciphered," he said.

Nyra set aside the first scroll and retrieved another one. The second bore runes similar in shape but arranged in looping patterns. "If these passages are correct, then an unbinding requires a crossweaving of runic inscriptions. Each set is carved or painted in a ring around the focus point—where you stand during the ritual." She ran her fingertip over a faint diagram. "We used some of these during the last attempt, but I think we missed a crucial piece that links them to your own blood and the wards within the fortress."

He studied her face. "Is that the reason we failed before?"

She hesitated. Her chest tightened with regret. "Possibly. Or perhaps we needed something else—another catalyst in addition to Emberleaf."

She noticed the tension flicker in his eyes at the mention of the elusive plant they needed. They had searched nearby slopes to no avail, but they'd located a small supply of the herb when the MerChain caravans came through the valley. She hoped it was enough.

"We will do everything we can with what we have," she added quickly. "That I can promise you."

She turned to a more detailed parchment, bracing it against a wooden rack so Rhezan could see it more easily.

A wave of relief passed through her when she realized the ink had not faded beyond recognition. "These runes are called spires," she said, pointing to a row of triangular shapes. "They are believed to magnify the wards in the walls, acting like channels for any magical energy shared by you and... me."

Her voice caught. She knew what it meant to rely on her own blood-magic again. It was still punishable by law, even though King Vorian and Rhezan had tolerated it for his sake. It would always be a risk, but looking at Rhezan's eyes, she found no hesitation there, only determination.

He brushed his claws lightly over the table's edge. The subtle scrape made her pulse jump. She often forgot how powerful he was, even in this reduced size. "You speak with such conviction," he said in a quiet rumble. "These runes, these shapes... do you truly believe they can free me from this prison?"

She swallowed and nodded, though she remained aware of the uncertainty swirling in her mind. "I do not see another way, and I refuse to abandon you to this fate."

His gaze turned inward, a flicker of something warm crossing his features. She realized he was on the verge of saying something else, but he closed his mouth, steadying himself. The unspoken words coiled between them, as tangible as the parchment on the table.

She fidgeted with the scroll's corners, pressing out tiny creases. The tension of the Great Hall seemed heightened by his presence. "I have a partial incantation," she ventured at last. "It references three main elements: the fortress wards, your draconic essence, and a bridging force." She tapped a line of text. "That bridging force might be my blood-magic. I see references to living essence... which is reminiscent of what we used before. But the instructions are incomplete. I need time to fill in the blanks."

Rhezan huffed softly, a calm exhale that ruffled the hair at her temples. "Time... we have too little of it."

She tried not to dwell on the outside threats pressing in on the kingdom. The rumor of war loomed, and the king had already insisted they hasten their efforts. She thought of Sera's arrival, of the uneasy tension that lingered any time the ambassador's name was mentioned. But she forced that thought away.

"Come closer," she said. She crouched on the stool, tilting one scroll outward. "Look at this symbol here—a series of interlocking crescents." She traced the curls with her fingertip, leaning in so she could position the parchment toward Rhezan's line of sight. A faint, smoky smell rose from the scroll whenever the firelight hit the old ink.

Before she realized it, her shoulder brushed against his scaled shoulder. Warmth radiated through the cloth of her sleeve, sending a flutter along her nerves. She became acutely aware of how near he was, how the flicker of torchlight caught every subtle shift of his obsidian scales. She drew in a breath. She was supposed to remain focused on the runes, yet her heart pounded with an altogether different tension.

"This is the formation we might need," she said, forcing her voice into a steady cadence. "If we shape the runes in these crescents around you, each ring will point to a different facet of the wards. We then weave them together with incantations that reference draconic essence. I believe that is the structure that will let me channel your power back into you, but in a purified state, free of the curse's corruption."

She became aware that Rhezan was no longer looking at the scroll. His gaze had shifted to her face. She felt a surge of heat beneath her cheeks, uncertain how to handle his intense scrutiny. She said nothing, letting the moment settle. A curious awareness crackled in the air between them.

At length, he drew back, clearing his throat in a low growl. "You have deciphered more than I realized."

Her lips formed a faint smile, though her pulse still hammered. "I have studied every scrap the library's shelves could spare. I am not finished either. Before we attempt anything, I want to be absolutely sure."

Rhezan nodded, though a flicker of impatience moved through his tail. She understood. He had lived under this curse for so long. Every day that passed likely felt like a blade against his resolve.

She tucked away the scroll with the crescents and drew another from the pile, one that had water stains along the edges. The words were nearly illegible in places. "This one might help fill in the incantation lulls. I have only translated the first section. It references a chain or a bond spike, something that may be the magical tether keeping you in this draconic form." She paused, biting her lip. "If I can identify that link, I can direct my magic to sever it."

She felt his breath hitch behind her. Turning slightly, she came face-to-face with his scaled muzzle. She tried to ignore the tiny prickle of fear that always surfaced when she thought about how easily his jaws could crush stone. But he had never threatened her in that way. His presence carried danger, yet also an unexpected sense of security, as though he would sooner burn every stone in the fortress than let her come to harm.

Her voice softened. "I know the risks. But if we want to break the curse, we must understand its exact shape. Once we do, it might be possible to unbind it fully."

He exhaled, lids half-lowering over his golden eyes. "You have accomplished more than all the others who came before you," he said. "Yet I still hunger for a solution."

Nyra looked at him. She remembered how, in many moments, his anger flared and overshadowed the man beneath the scales. The frustration in his voice now was raw rather than explosive.

"I promise you, we will keep pushing," she whispered. "We will find the missing pieces. We will free you."

He said nothing at first, only continued to watch her, gaze flicking from her hair to her hands braced on the scroll. She felt that same strange flutter, a sense that something was building between them that had little to do with forbidden runes. The heavy timbre of his voice broke the quiet.

"Nyra..." he began, then fell silent again.

Everything seemed to pause. The roar of the hearth, the distant bustle of the fortress staff, the hint of wind beyond the tall doors—all of it faded in importance. She swallowed, wanting to ask him what weighed so heavily on his mind. But she let him find the words for himself.

Instead, she offered him a small nod, as though granting permission for him to speak freely. Suddenly, he closed his jaw, wings shifting slightly as he turned an intent focus on the parchment. She read his change in posture with a pang of disappointment. It was almost as if he had been on the verge of sharing something deeply personal, only to retreat.

Refusing to linger on that letdown, she gave a gentle clap of her hands. "Would you like me to go through any of these passages again?" She attempted a lighter tone, though her heart still hammered from the close proximity they had shared.

Rhezan drew in a steady breath, blinking to clear some hidden thought. "Yes," he said quietly. "Review the portion about bridging your magic with my own. I want to be certain I understand. I do not want to risk another incomplete attempt. Last time, the consequences..." His jaw tightened, recalling the pain that had nearly unmanned him.

She winced, remembering how he had collapsed, halfway lost between draconic power and a brief glimpse of human form. "No repeats," she murmured. "I will do whatever I must to ensure it works next time."

She eased onto the stool again, this time leaning over a different scroll that contained more robust linework describing a ritual circle. As she did, she noticed how close she was to Rhezan once more. The heat from his scales was undeniable, a low-grade warmth that caressed her skin. When her shoulder brushed against him again, she did not move away. She could feel the strong rhythm of his heartbeat through that hardened exterior, steady and insistent.

SEVENTEEN

Later that night, in bed, Nyra's eyes refused to close. For one more endless night, she stared at the shifting shadows across the walls of her chamber, heart pounding in a rhythm of restlessness. Two low-burning candles on the small table provided meager light, illuminating the stack of parchment on which she had meticulously sketched runes. Those same runes, newly carved in Rhezan's cursed cavern, beckoned her mind to churn. She had spent weeks honing their shapes next to the sinister glyphs etched by whoever had cursed the prince so long ago. Despite her exhaustive effort, uncertainty clung to her thoughts.

She pushed aside the blankets and sat up, letting the chill of the air nip at her bare arms. She had grown accustomed to the fortress's cold, but tonight it seemed sharper than usual, knife-like against her skin. She pulled a thin robe around her shoulders, feeling her nerves prickle with unresolved tension. On the small table lay her scattered notes about the rumored armies amassing beyond the mountains. Whispers around the corridors said rival realms did not believe a single word the king had shared about his son's health. They assumed the Dragon Prince was too weak, rumored to be half dead from an unhealed wound. The fortress staff kept repeating that war seemed inevitable, and no matter how intensely Nyra pored over possible rituals, it did not change the fact that an enemy invasion could be close at hand.

A sliver of moonlight crept through the narrow window, reflecting off her notes. Unable to sit still, she took a breath and stood. Wandering might lull her thoughts enough to chase away the looming fears that made her chest feel tightened by some invisible band. She slipped on her sturdy boots and dressing gown, then knocked on the door. They were still keeping her under lock and key which was damn irritating, but she hadn't won her freedom yet. That wouldn't come until she lifted Rhezan's curse.

The door opened and the guard stationed at her door gave her a slight nod then followed her as she padded down the hallway. The guards had gotten used to her roaming the castle on occasion when she couldn't sleep and she never went anywhere that was forbidden to her anyway.

The corridors were hushed and flickered with the light of occasional torches. The thick stone arches above gave everything a vaulted echo that made footsteps seem unnaturally loud. She suppressed the urge to tiptoe. After all, secrecy was not truly her aim. She only needed space to think. Her mind flicked back to the runes in the cavern. They were delicate lines that might channel her blood-magic more precisely, or at least so she hoped. But the question rattling her thoughts was far more intense than where to place the next curve. She feared that, if she pressed forward with more blood-based spells, she would be labeled a traitor in the king's court.

She paused by a window embrasure overlooking an internal courtyard. Her breath caught at the sight of the fortress as it stretched upward into a star-flecked sky. Tucked behind tall spires, she spotted a winged silhouette in the highest turret, outlined faintly against the moon-light. Her heart twisted because there was only possibility who it might be. Few roamed the fortress at midnight, and she suspected Rhezan's presence was as restless as hers.

She decided to climb the stairs that spiraled to the turret. Clenching the folds of her robe tighter around her, she started up the steps, letting the quiet swirl around her. Each footstep landed with muffled assurance on the worn stones. She felt a heightened awareness tingle in her chest. In truth, she had not spoken to Rhezan at length these last few days. He had been distant, as though consumed by his own worries.

Reaching the top, she eased open a creaking wooden door. A breeze brushed her cheeks, making her exhale in a shudder. The turret's platform was not large, but it offered a breathtaking panorama of the mountains' jagged outlines and the faint pinpricks of starlight. High above, the moon hung pale and cool, casting silver over every-thing in sight.

Rhezan stood near the edge, his stance subtle in the gloom. Moonlight traced the edges of his dragon form, his massive wings were tucked into his body. His obsidian scales were not as large as his full draconic shape, yet he was far larger than a typical man. He must have been in the smaller dragon form he often adopted when he wanted to move about the corridors. A faint glow of molten gold-colored his gaze when he turned and noticed her.

In that quiet moment, neither of them spoke. The wind sighed along the parapets, stirring the loose folds of her robe and shifting the fringe of her hair as it brushed across her brow. She took a hesitant step forward, mindful that one sudden sound might shatter the fragile hush.

"Could you not sleep?" she asked, her voice just above a whisper.

His wings twitched slightly. "No," he answered in a low rumble. "There is too much on my mind."

She exhaled, moving closer until she could rest her hands on the cold stone battlement. Below, the courtyard lay silent, its cobblestones washed in moonlight. For a moment, they stood side by side, neither quite looking at the other, both allowing the breeze to carry tension away.

"Rumors are everywhere," she said, voicing the thought that weighed on her heart. "I hear that the surrounding realms do not believe your father's attempts to reassure them of your strength. They say King Vorian is desperate, that he would say anything to maintain his throne. The gossip claims war could break out at any moment."

Rhezan's jaw tensed, the outline of his fangs visible when he spoke. "I know. The king sent out letters, official notices, even envoys. Yet no one trusts an aging ruler with an heir locked in a dragon's body. They suspect we are vulnerable. I can feel the tension from the soldiers, the staff, everyone inside this hold."

Nyra nodded, sliding her palm along the cold stone. "I am afraid that, if I fail to cure you, the fortress will fall under siege. And even if I succeed in curing you with my magic, there is still a chance your father's privy council will brand me a traitor for using forbidden magic."

His molten gaze flickered toward her. "Why do you say that?"

She attempted a small, humorless laugh. "Because it is outlawed. Blood-magic is the reason your father's councilors watch me so closely. Some refuse to believe I can use it for anything good. They only endure it now because you once told them you permitted it. No one else in the realm has that authority, but the king and his close advisors are desperate."

Rhezan lifted one powerful foreleg, claws scraping gently on the stone. "They need your forbidden skills, and they blame you for having them in the first place. King Vorian's acceptance is conditional. If the time comes when the fortress is threatened from outside and they require a scapegoat, you wonder if they might place the blame on your magic."

His words turned her blood cold because that fear had haunted her every sleepless hour. She felt a knot tighten in her chest. "Yes," she managed. "And if war ignites, they will want someone to condemn. I already sense councilors whispering that your father is allowing horrifying sorceries within these walls. They may see me as a convenient target."

Rhezan's tail gave a slow, deliberate swish. For a moment, she heard the faint scrape of scales against stone. He looked out across the mountain range illuminated by moonlight. The slope of his back caught the pale glow, revealing the ridges and lines of old scars. Though he rarely spoke of it, she knew how many times he had been hunted or wounded because of the curse.

"They cannot blame you alone," he said softly. "I agreed to your methods. If the worst happens, I will remind them you saved my life."

Nyra's throat constricted with emotion. She kept her gaze forward, watching the clouds drifting past the moon. She had rarely heard him sound so resolute when defending her from the possibility of condemnation.

"Thank you," she said. "Though if war is truly at our doorstep, your father might not be able to protect either of us."

Rhezan let out a quiet sigh. "I know. My father tries valiantly to maintain order. But these realms, especially the ones that once feared our power, are hungry for any sign of weakness." He paused, eyes distant. "For generations, people viewed dragons as monstrous, unstoppable weapons. Perhaps a part of me is monstrous. I was reminded of that by many who visited in the early years of my curse."

Her heart twisted at the sadness in his voice. She

turned fully toward him, letting the breeze ruffle her hair. "You are not a monster," she said firmly. "You are cursed. It is different."

His gaze flickered with bitter memory. "Others did not see it that way. They saw a dragon, feared me, and expected that no trace of the man I was remained beneath the scales. Some tried to befriend me for political gain. Others tried to kill me, hoping to make a trophy of my head. I tasted more betrayals than acts of mercy."

He lowered his head until she glimpsed the faint ridges that formed the top of his snout. When he spoke again, she heard a subtle tremor of hurt. "That is why your help confuses me so. You stand here with me, risking your life for a possibility you cannot guarantee. I cannot tell if you are fearless or hopelessly stubborn."

She smiled faintly, though sorrow etched the corners of her eyes. "It might be both," she confessed. "I refuse to ignore suffering if I have the power to help, no matter the cost."

He lifted his gaze to hers. In the hush of the night, the depth of his gold eyes made her breath catch. The wind against the tower's stone curves carried a low whistle, weaving around them in an odd lullaby.

"I wish I had your certainty," he murmured. "The betrayals I endured poisoned my trust in most humans. My own curse is the proof that words can be twisted and loves can be shattered for political convenience. Even now, the memory of it keeps a barrier around my heart."

Nyra remembered the shape of the runes that had bound him, the raw anguish etched into his posture every time the curse flared. She thought of Ambassador Sera, who had once been close to him before the affliction. The heartbreak he suffered was still plain in every guarded look.

"You are not alone," she said softly. "I cannot change your past, and I cannot promise the next attempt in casting the ritual will work. But I can stand beside you... if you will let me."

A shiver ran through Rhezan, a subtle tremor that shifted his wings. The next breath he took sounded ragged. "I keep telling myself not to rely on you, that trusting again will only open old wounds. Yet you have shown me kindness that I long thought impossible."

Her eyes grew misty. She bowed her head slightly, as if to acknowledge the weight of his words. Silence returned, heavy with unspoken confessions that hovered in the air. She could feel the tension coil inside her as well, a swirl of uncertainty about what would become of them both.

Around them, the star-filled sky seemed impossibly vast. The wind carried a faint tang of pine from some-where along the mountain pass. Nyra's pulse pounded in her ears, her shoulders tense from the day's labor in the dark caverns. She recalled each rune she had carved, each symbol etched into stone with the hope of severing the curse that imprisoned this prince.

She reached out, her hand trembling slightly as it hovered near Rhezan's foreleg. The raised obsidian scales felt cool at first touch. When she laid her palm there, she was surprised by how his warmth surged through the surface. In that quiet moment, it felt like an unspoken apology, a wordless promise that she would try to be strong enough for both of them.

"I understand what's at stake for me," she whispered, "I either lift your curse and be a hero, or fail and probably be thrown into the dungeons to rot. I only know one thing for sure: I must try to heal you."

His chest rose and fell in a heavy sigh. "If the ritual fails...again...and war breaks out, the privy council might make you the scapegoat. The irony is that, even if you succeed, some might fear your magic more than they fear an army at the gates."

She squeezed her eyes shut, letting the weight of that truth sink in. He was right. No matter which path unfolded, her blood-magic would remain a point of controversy. Yet giving up on Rhezan was not an option in her heart.

"I understand," she said. "I will accept the risk, because I believe your life is worth saving."

He turned his giant head, stepping closer. She felt the closeness of his scaled flank, the warmth of his breath as it brushed her hair. They stood so near that the slightest shift would bring them fully together. Then, almost hesitantly, he lifted one foreleg awkwardly, as if searching for a position to offer comfort. She realized this old fortress had shaped his entire sense of self, had given him too few chances to offer any gentleness.

She stepped closer in response, letting the curve of her shoulder rest against his scaled arm. The contact felt precarious, neither entirely fitting nor entirely foreign. Tension hummed through the small space between them, but something else arose too. It felt like a shared isolation, a bond of two souls pressed beneath the weight of unrelenting expectation.

They stayed like that, letting the night sky above the tower enfold them. The quiet around them bore witness to the unspoken emotions gleaned from each other's measured breaths. The turret's walls loomed as silent sentinels, and the narrow parapet behind them gave an impression that the rest of the world had faded.

Nyra's eyes pricked with tears she did not let fall. She felt the low rumble in his chest, not quite a growl, more like an unsteady exhale struggling to become words. She knew that each betrayal he had endured still haunted him, as her own losses haunted her. And in that moment, she wanted to tell him that she did not fear the monstrous shape he wore, or the war that threatened them both. She feared losing the fragile connection they had only begun to build.

She forced her eyes open, swallowing the thickness in her throat. "Rhezan," she whispered, "I cannot predict everything that awaits us, but I will do whatever it takes to see you freed from this ordeal. Not only because your people need you, but because... I believe in you."

His reply came in a trembling rumble. "You share more faith in me than I have in myself."

She let her cheek graze his scales, acceptance moving gently between them. She thought of the days when she first arrived, when he roared at her from the cavern shadows and she thought all hope was lost. Now, the distance between them was shorter than the space of an inhale.

He lowered his head, and she felt the light press of his snout against her shoulder. It was a tentative, careful embrace unlike any she had known, a quiet expression of mutual solace. Her hands rose, one resting on the side of his neck. The ridges of his scales met her fingertips, and she realized that beneath the hardened exterior, she felt the faint thump of his heartbeat.

They stood in that quiet, exchanging no further words. For a moment, it was enough. The fortress below them seemed to hold its breath, uncertain of the future. They faced the sky, the mountains, and the intangible promise of all that might unfold. Even with their hearts weighed down by looming war and potential condemnation, this small contact felt like an anchor, a momentary refuge.

At last, a gust of wind rattled the turret, and the chill squeezed between them. Reluctantly, Nyra drew back. She met his gaze, seeing in his golden eyes a profound exhaustion and the first shadows of renewed hope.

"We should get some rest," she said, her voice quiet. "Tomorrow I must verify the runes. Perhaps my new adjustments will strengthen our next attempt to break the curse."

He nodded. His tail twitched as if acknowledging her plan without needing to speak. She sensed how much he embraced the possibility of relief in her rituals, even if he feared the cost.

She stepped backward from the parapet, letting her hand slip away from his scales. He curled his wings closer to his body, grief and longing crisscrossing his features in the silvery moonlight. In her chest, she felt a strange ache at the distance that returned as soon as their connection ended.

A moment later, a steward hurried through the archway, his boots skidding slightly on the stone. "Lady Nyra!" he panted, breathless but grinning. "Councilor Jori just received a parcel from the Merchain Express—one of the herbal traders had it after all. It's Emberleaf. A full bundle, freshly sealed."

Nyra's heart skipped. Hope flared like flint on tinder and she thought she might weep with joy.

EIGHTEEN

Rhezan's wings trembled with suppressed nerves, and his chest felt tight, as though he was sucking air through a thin tube. Torchlight flickered against the cavern walls, each flame throwing jagged shadows across the runes Nyra had carved. The circle of markings glowed with an eerie light, reflecting on his obsidian scales. His gaze shifted to the upper shelf of rock where his father, King Vorian, Harmond, and Jori watched him, their arms crossed over their chests and scowls on their faces.

He knew they had chosen that spot for a reason. He was unpredictable when in pain. Fire had a way of escaping him when he wasn't fully in control. He understood their caution, though the knowledge of it stung. There was a part of him who was still a boy wanting his father near when he was in pain.

When Nyra stepped to his side, he dared to lower his head so she could reach him. Her presence steadied him. Her apron pockets bulged with herbs. She looked at him with serious eyes. He knew she had prepared for this moment with everything she possessed. It made him want to trust the uncertain path ahead.

She raised her voice softly. "You are certain you want to begin now?"

He took a steady breath. His voice rolled out, deep and rumbling, echoing against the curved cavern walls. "Yes. There is no point in waiting any longer." He paused, feeling a claw graze the stone. "If there is a chance I can reclaim my humanity, I want to take it. No matter the risk."

A faint tremor passed through his limbs, but he tried to hide it. Harmond and Jori whispered to each other, their words too muted to pick out, but he sensed their anxiety. King Vorian's gaze never left Rhezan's face, as though bracing himself for any outcome.

Nyra reached up to place her hand on one of his thick forelegs. The warmth of her palm seeped into his scales. Her voice was gentle. "I will ask you to sit in the center here." She gestured to the middle of the runes and stepped sideways, giving him space. "You must keep as still as possible, at least at the start."

Barely inhaling, Rhezan shuffled forward, each step creating a metallic clink from the shackles that lay coiled at his feet. The heavy chains rattled ominously when he settled. A servant with a guarded expression hurried to anchor each cuff around his limbs. Rhezan forced his wings to stay tight against his back, though his muscles quivered. The echo of steel scraping rock set his teeth on edge.

He glanced at Nyra again and lowered his voice so only she could hear. "Will it hurt?" he asked, though he knew the answer. He wanted reassurance, and he almost regretted asking.

Nyra's expression tightened in empathy. "When the curse first took hold, it hurt you, right?"

He recalled that scorching pain, which had torn him out of his old life and forced him into scales and talons. "Yes," he said, voice flat. "It felt like my body was splitting apart."

She swallowed. Soft sorrow darkened her eyes. "I expect it will hurt this time as well. We do not have a gentle way to tear you free of the dark magic that witch used on you. I wish it were otherwise."

He nodded, a slow, tense dip of his great head. The weight of old dread pressed on him. "Then I am ready. I would rather endure agony than remain a monster."

Nyra exhaled through parted lips, as though rallying her own resolve. "You must hold onto that intention," she said. "Your mind will need it when the pain comes. If you try to fight the shift mid-process—"

"I will face it," he said, firmly. "Finish what you must do."

She gave a solemn nod, then turned to gather her supplies. The cave grew colder in that moment, or perhaps it was only Rhezan's nerves. Distantly, a guard to the side of the cavern lit another torch, and shadowy corners leapt into brightness. He heard the rustle of a scroll, the clank of metal, the faint breath of the king as he shifted his stance overhead.

Nyra moved swiftly. She arranged the small stone bowl on the floor near Rhezan's snout. She poured a shimmering mixture of crushed herbs, including the precious Emberleaf, into it. The pungent smell of the new herb mix reminded him of pine resin and something far sharper... almost a hint of sulpher. She added into the bowl glowing liquid from a vial, then swirled the liquid around until it formed thick rivulets. Finally, she peered up at him.

"Drink as much of this as you can," she said. "I have prepared it to calm your body and open your natural magic flow. It will help bind the runes. After that, we move on to the rest."

He lowered his muzzle, drawing in a hollow breath before extending his tongue to lap at the bowl's contents. At once, heat traveled from his tongue to the back of his mouth. He drank until his throat burned, and the first sparks of dizziness hit him. He growled softly, forcing himself to keep going. When the bowl was near empty, he pulled his head back, swallowing repeatedly.

Above, the privy councilors edged closer. Harmond spoke in a clipped tone that echoed faintly. "My Lord King, is it wise to continue?"

Rhezan's father returned a grim reply. Rhezan's ears, though scaled and pointed, struggled to parse the exact words. He felt the potion swirl in his veins, robbing him of the ability to focus on anything but Nyra's next steps. He forced himself to keep breathing. The thick weight of the chains reminded him of his vow: he would see this through, no matter how brutal it felt.

Nyra lifted a small curved blade and pressed the edge

against her palm. Rhezan tensed at the sight. The stale air thickened with the scent of copper when the blade bit her skin. She uttered a harsh exhale, then pulled her hand away, a line of red trickling down her wrist.

She pressed her palm to the runes carved along the walls, smearing her blood in brisk, deliberate strokes. The lines glowed, flickering like candle flames caught in a gust. The entire chamber seemed to hum, a low note that rattled the stone beneath Rhezan's claws. His wings gave another involuntary shiver.

Nyra began chanting. Her words, part incantation and part fervent plea, undulated in the heavy cave air. Runes glimmered in response, each stroke lighting up with an otherworldly glow. The swirling shapes on the walls reminded Rhezan of an ancient script that once bound him, now repurposed to free him. He squeezed his eyes shut, bracing for the inevitable.

His body went rigid when the magic bit through his scales. A sudden spike of white-hot heat tore across his spine. He roared, the sound crashing through the cave. The chains rattled as he jerked back, the agony unlike any ordinary wound. It was deep magic, ripping at the core of his being.

He breathed fire, most of it ferociously licked the floor thirty feet in front of him. The king and councilors leapt behind the rocks. He heard them shout overhead, but the sounds blurred. Right now, he heard only Nyra's voice chanting over the rush of his own blood. Every syllable pulsed in time with his heartbeat. Her incantation rose in volume, straining over his roars.

The magic crackled through every scale. Pain coalesced in his limbs, forging a relentless ache that thumped in time with the runic glow. He roared again and felt the walls tremble. He tested the chains, claws scraping the floor. They held.

His mind threatened to slip. Memories flashed: the day the curse first consumed him, the betrayal of old acquaintances. The searing heartbreak he had carried. He tried to anchor himself to hope. Yes, he reminded himself, if I survive this, I might be free. The incantation buzzed in his skull, and he clung to Nyra's presence with whatever willpower he had left.

Above him, the runes flickered. In his haze, he noticed them dimming, then flaring to life. Nyra's voice cracked, but she kept chanting, pushing harder, her blood still staining the stone. Rhezan panted. Fire burned at the back of his throat as he tried to remain still. The entire cave seemed to spin.

Gradually, a shift rippled down his spine. He felt the chains drop looser around him. He gasped at the realization that his body was shrinking. In the bright glow of the runes, his mighty limbs began to recede. He coughed, falling to a knee as new shapes took hold. The chains clattered against him, sliding across newly narrow shoulders.

For an instant, his perspective changed. He blinked, no longer forced to crane his neck to see the walls. He was in that smaller draconic shape he had sometimes used. His vision blurred at the edges, but he caught sight of Nyra, sweat streaming down her face. Her eyes shone with determination. She pressed her bloody hand to another carved symbol.

He tried to speak, but only a strained rasp emerged from his draconic throat. She shouted something back, voice ragged, continuing the chant. Then the lines on the wall started to dance, flickering like a dying torch in gusty wind. A sudden wave of energy surged. Rhezan's limbs spasmed, and he felt a wave of uncontrolled trembling swarm over him.

He lurched sideways. This time, the shift felt more severe. Pain hammered beneath his skin, forcing him to close his eyes again. Through the haze, he sensed something changing at the core of his bones. A brief, glorious moment of relief flooded him. He gasped, feeling a cool breeze on skin rather than scales. He was almost human. One chain slipped, scraping his thigh. He realized, dazed, he had human legs again, hands instead of claws. His chest rose and fell with panicked breaths.

He opened his eyes just long enough to see Nyra crouched near him. She looked on the verge of tears, chanting with renewed desperation. Her voice surged, and the runes flared bright green. Something about the color chilled him, reminding him of curses older than any mortal knowledge. Then, all at once, the brightness clawed him back.

He cried out as the cursed magic whipped through his shape. Scales exploded across his arms and shoulders. In one heartbeat, the human part vanished, replaced by his larger dragon form. He heard his father shout, possibly calling his name. The renewed agony slammed him to the ground, and he roared. His wings convulsed, toppling a torch stand. Sparks rained over the floor but fizzled in the swirl of Nyra's magic.

The entire chamber plunged into chaos. The runes on the wall flared in shades of green and red and black and blue with frantic inconsistency. Nyra's chant escalated, but something was unravelling in the magic. Rhezan could hardly focus. He only knew the pain was overwhelming. He felt each tendon re-forming into a monstrous shape, the half-healed curse snapping back into place.

He staggered a final time, still chained, yet large enough again to fill much of the cave's center. A green light burst at his periphery, and he roared in torment. Then the light cut out, leaving him shuddering. With a final, ragged cry, his limbs gave way. He collapsed onto his side, gasping. Darkness crept around the edges of his vision. For a breath, he could not gather enough air to speak. His body felt pinned by an immense weight. The taste of blood and ash clung to his tongue.

A stunned silence seized the cavern.

High above, King Vorian's alarmed voice echoed. Rhezan was too dizzy to decipher the words. He only saw Nyra's silhouette in the torchlight, stumbling toward him. Her free hand touched his scales, searching for a sign that he still breathed. She caught her breath in a sob, her shoulders trembling.

Rhezan tried to speak, but a jolt of weakness flooded him. The sharp tang of failure weighed on him in those final seconds of awareness. His vision blurred, and his body felt impossibly heavy. He felt the stone beneath his side, heard the clank of chains tangling around him. Somewhere above, footsteps pounded along the outcropping. A new voice, furious and unwavering, rang out across the cavern.

Nyra jerked her gaze up. A tall, raven-haired woman stood beside the king's, glowering down into the ritual space. Her robes shimmered with embroidered designs that caught the torchlight. Rage twisted her expression as she looked from the bloodied runes to Nyra's knife, then to Rhezan's half-conscious form.

"What is the meaning of this?" the woman shouted in a clipped, resonant tone. Her words echoed off the walls, thick with accusation. "Blood-magic is forbidden, and you are killing Prince Rhezan!"

Nyra's backbone went rigid. Rhezan saw her face go pale, but he could not muster the strength to respond. The pain in his body was too great, and darkness closed over his vision. The final thing Rhezan heard was the echo of that condemning voice reverberate through the hollow stone expanse.

CHAPTER

NINETEEN

Nyra's heartbeat pounded as she bent over Rhezan's massive form sprawled across the cave floor. Her surroundings felt dreamlike, as though every sound reached her through a haze. The chamber still smelled of charred incense and the bitter tang of magic gone awry. Fragments of greenish light flickered and died on the runes carved into the damp stone walls. The runes were meant to help her break his curse. Instead, they had gone dark and left Rhezan unconscious.

She pressed both palms to his side, feeling the smooth plane of his black scales. When her fingers registered the faint stir of breath, she forced herself to exhale. He was alive. His flank rose and fell, so shallow she feared it might fade altogether at any second. She swallowed a knot of dread. Her own blood, still wet from the cuts on her palms, had smeared across his shoulders and the rocky ground. She had channeled that blood into the ritual mere

209

moments ago. Everything had collapsed into chaos before she could finish.

Voices and thudding footsteps echoed nearby. High above her, on a rocky outcropping built into the cavern's wall, the king, the privy councilors, and Ambassador Sera had witnessed the failure from a distance. The manacles that once circled Rhezan's forelegs now lay twisted. At some point, as the magic raged, the chains had loosened under his thrashing until they were left in a scraggly heap of metal. Their clanking still resonated in the back of Nyra's mind, mingling with the memory of Rhezan's tortured roars.

"Stay with me," she whispered, leaning closer to his scaled head. She could not imagine how awful it must have felt to be pulled in and out of his mortal skin with the curse tearing at him. She wanted to see him awake, hear him speak in that low voice that once rumbled with subdued torment. Now, he made no sound at all.

A sharper clamor of voices overhead snapped her out of her daze. She glanced upward to view the King Vorian descending the steep steps from that stone ledge. He rushed forward with a vigor that betrayed his age. Harmond and Jori followed, alarmed. Right behind them, the dark-haired woman navigated the rocky slope with an air of authority. She wore finely embroidered robes that glimmered even in the uneven torchlight, and she carried herself as though used to having people leap aside at her approach. Nyra guessed this woman had to be Ambassador Sera, the one who had arrived just as the ritual collapsed.

Nyra stayed crouched by Rhezan's side, one hand resting gently along the slope of his neck. "Do not die on me," she mouthed softly, offering a plea more than a command. Her legs shook with exhaustion, and she tasted copper on her tongue. She had poured enormous effort into chanting, controlling her own blood, and steadying the wards she had hoped to harness. Instead, she was left shivering on the cold stone with streaks of her life's essence trailing down her arms.

The group raced across the cavern floor, boots crunching on grit and broken shards of old runic stone. King Vorian's emerald cloak dragged behind him, edges catching the dust. The tall woman's presence loomed over everyone else's, posture rigid, eyes flashing with barely contained fury. Nyra braced herself for confrontation, but she refused to move away from Rhezan to greet them. Someone had to keep watch over him, in case his breathing faltered.

"You," the raven-haired woman said, pointing at Nyra with a trembling hand. "You have all but murdered him. What in every corner of the realm were you thinking?" Her voice cut sharply, echoing through the cavern with a ferocity that matched the anger twisting in her features.

Nyra lifted her gaze, body tensed. "I was doing what was necessary." Her own tone wavered from a mixture of heartbreak and defiance. "He wanted this ritual."

"Blood-magic," Sera spat, eyes narrowing in disgust. "Whose brilliant idea was that?"

King Vorian stepped between them, turning to fix Sera with a grave stare. "I allowed this. I approved of whatever method might help my son, Ambassador." His voice resonated with quiet steel. "We all want him cured."

Sera's scowl deepened, but she took a moment to measure the king's expression before she spoke again. When she finally addressed him, each word vibrated with impatience. "Forgive me if I sound furious, my liege, but this looks exactly like an abomination. Look at him." She motioned toward Rhezan. "He is lying there unconscious and might not wake up."

Nyra flinched. She felt each syllable lance through her. She forced down the urge to snap. Instead, she placed her right palm tentatively over Rhezan's chest, searching for the thud of his heartbeat beneath the scales.

King Vorian did not break Sera's gaze. "We made the decision to attempt this ritual. The entire council agreed to it if my son consented. And he did."

The two privy councilors, who had reached the space behind the king's shoulder, nodded in anxious harmony. Their eyes flickered from Rhezan to Sera and back again.

Sera gave a low hiss of frustration. "Then everyone here bears blame for this madness. Blood-magic is not a plaything. I spent a lifetime fighting against illicit spells, and now I arrive to find you encouraging them?"

"That is quite enough." King Vorian's voice chilled the air. His posture straightened, thick silver hair catching the ambient torchlight. "I respect your counsel, Ambassador Sera, but remember who wears the crown."

She pursed her lips, her posture rigid. "I apologize for my outburst, my king," she began, in a tone that implied she felt anything but remorse. "However, I must express my complete outrage and disapproval. Blood-magic kills. We do not see the kind of destruction it can leave behind until it is too late."

At that, a dark flicker of pain rose in Nyra's chest. She lifted her chin, meeting the other woman's accusatory stare. "Rhezan is not dead," she said, voice trembling with intensity. "He is alive, and he chose this path himself." She hoped no one could see her hands shake. She clenched them into fists, ignoring the sting of her open cut. "He agreed to every step. I explained the risks."

Sera let out a disdainful scoff. "He is out cold on that cavern floor. How can you claim the risk was worth it when we see no success?"

Nyra's anger pierced the raw ache of disappointment she already felt. She rose from her kneeling position, mindful to keep one hand on Rhezan's side as though to protect him from her adversary's words. "The ritual showed a moment of promise. He had human limbs for a few breaths. If the wards had not faltered, if the draconic essence had not fought back, perhaps," she said, her voice catching, "we might have broken the curse. This was never guaranteed to be painless or simple. You cannot uproot deep magic in a tranquil manner."

One of the privy councilors softly cleared his throat. "We saw him shrink down, and becom ehuman if only for an instant. Then something snapped back. It was," he hesitated, "it was dreadful to watch."

"There could be errors in my runes," Nyra continued. "Or maybe I missed a crucial ingredient to stabilize it all." She shook her head, dizzy with the swirl of possibilities.

The exhaustion of channeling blood-magic still weighed on her limbs. "I just know one thing: He is alive, and I will find a way to bring him back to consciousness."

Sera's lip curled faintly, though she kept her tone measured now that the king had instructed her to contain herself. "I truly want the curse lifted," she said, gesturing at Rhezan's immense body. "I want him freed as much as any loyal subject, but not at the cost of his life. That is what I question. The same power you used to blow the wards wide open might ensure his permanent destruction next time."

Before Nyra could counter, King Vorian exhaled, heavy with the toll of the night's events. "Ambassador Sera," he said, "your words are heard. Yet I must remind you that, until we see conclusive results, you are in no position to override my command. Nyra's methods have saved my son's life once before. If we do not try every route possible, this curse will consume him forever."

Sera drummed her nails on the small metal clasp of her cloak. "I was brought back here because His Majesty's council called me home. I do not intend to let my experience go unused." She flicked a glare at Nyra that nearly seared. "But neither do I intend to watch the prince be ground to dust beneath the weight of this... questionable sorcery."

Nyra felt a slow burn behind her eyelids. She refused to show weakness in front of this woman. "Rhezan wanted me to see it through." She balled her hands tighter. Blood from her palm smeared across pieces of broken chain. "He and I discussed that the cost might be high, but I was not about to withhold the most powerful weapon in my healing arsenal. If you actually want him saved, you will stop demeaning my methods and help me figure out what failed."

The only sounds in the cave were the low hiss from a torch sputtering on the far wall and the ragged hush of Rhezan's breath. His scaled chest rose again in a shallow motion. The relief of seeing that gave Nyra renewed strength. She knelt, ignoring the sharp ache in her knees, and pressed her palm on his neck to feel for his pulse. She listened to the magic within her and, in seconds, she felt his heart. The beat was faint and slow but present.

King Vorian lowered himself to a crouch on Rhezan's other side. His gaze was locked on his son's unconscious form, lines of worry etched deep into his brow. "Can you revive him, even if the curse remains?" he asked, voice quietly urgent. "Do you have anything in that bag of yours to wake him, or at least confirm he is stable?"

Nyra nodded. "I have a potion that might help ease any residual impact from the shifting magic. He is in his dragon shape, which complicates things. But if I can coax him to swallow even a small amount, it could restore him enough to wake." She swallowed. "I will do everything I can to make sure he recovers."

Sera's voice cut in, calmer but still laced with scorn. "What if your potions fail? What if he never opens his eyes again? Or if he does, but the curse tightens its hold?"

Nyra rose once more, struggling to keep bitterness from overwhelming her. "If you truly want him free, you would respect the process enough not to undermine it at every turn," she declared. Tears threatened her composure. "I know the risk. Rhezan knew it as well. He explicitly told me to see this through."

Sera turned her glare upon King Vorian. "Why did you allow her to risk your son's life like this? You are the king. Surely you have the power to forbid such reckless magic if you wished."

He stood slowly, shoulders squaring. His face darkened like he was a storm and he was about to sweep Sera off the face of the Earth. "You dare to question me? It is only because you have served me so well, for so long, that I do not throw you into a jail cell right now. I permitted it because I believe it may succeed." His eyes were darker in the flickering torchlight. "Rhezan himself urged me to let Nyra do whatever it took. Blood-magic or not, that was his choice. I grant him the agency to decide. He may be bound in this wretched form, but he is still my son."

Sera pressed her lips together so tightly they thinned to a pale line. For an instant, her features softened, betraying a genuine pang of concern for Rhezan. She glanced away and said in a quieter voice, "I care about him too." Then she pulled her shoulders back and let her gaze return to Nyra. "However, I do not trust your brand of magic."

Nyra felt a flicker of sympathy, but it vanished as soon as she recalled the scorn in Sera's voice. "If you cared, you would not undermine him," she stated. "He made the call to attempt the ritual even though it might transform him painfully. We almost succeeded. I only need time to discover which part of the incantation faltered. I need to see if the wards here in the cave reacted badly to my blood."

Harmond stepped forward, clearing his throat again. "We should take small steps. The immediate concern is that the prince stays alive. We cannot achieve anything if he does not wake."

Nyra avoided looking at Sera. She forced herself to adopt a more clinical tone. "I agree. First, I will do what I can to restore him to consciousness. Then I will examine the runes and figure out if we simply didn't have enough. Or maybe there was a mis alignment of the runes. I am not sure."

Sera studied her with a resentful calm. "If you want my assistance, I will be with the king, ensuring no further harm comes to Rhezan. But I will not stand back if I see your monstrous spell is devouring what is left of him."

Nyra's tears finally escaped their careful leash, trickling hot down her cheeks. She gave a tremulous nod, choosing not to hurl more words. Standing by Rhezan's side, she ran a shaky hand over his neck, brushing a portion of his obsidian scales. She could almost imagine him stirring and rasping out a sarcastic remark about petty squabbles, as he sometimes did before.

King Vorian moved around Rhezan's flank, gently placing a hand near Nyra's. "Do what you must," he said, voice thick. "I will keep the court at bay if that is what you need."

"I appreciate that, Your Majesty," she whispered. The truth remained that she was drained both physically and emotionally, yet her determination kindled anew. She owed it to Rhezan to stand strong. They had come too far to give up.

Sera's icy stare slid across Nyra, leaving a chill behind. "We will see if your vow to save him holds. For now, I will secure additional support," she said. She pivoted on her heel to address the king, ignoring Nyra entirely. "My expertise may aid in verifying the wards around this cave. We cannot risk a second attempt without analyzing what happened."

King Vorian inclined his head. "Take whichever route you see fit, Ambassador. But never forget that Rhezan's well-being is our priority."

The ambassador nodded stiffly. Then she shot Nyra a final glare. "We will talk more, Healer, once you have calmed yourself. Do not presume every eye in this fortress trusts you."

Nyra let out a shuddering breath as Sera stepped back from the group. The tension rolling off her in waves felt potent enough to quench the nearest torch. It took another full minute of uneasy quiet for the group to settle into a loose half-circle around Rhezan and Nyra.

The king, still kneeling, murmured to one of the privy councilors, an older man with worry lines etched into his brow. Nyra stayed tuned to the faint rhythm of Rhezan's breathing. As long as that subtle rise and fall remained, she would not yield to panic.

Finally, Sera spoke again, her voice brittle, but less loud than before. "Let me see if I can interpret anything from these runes," she announced, stepping toward the wall. "It might help us glean how badly the blood-magic disrupted them."

Nyra sensed Sera's every movement even with her back half-turned. She fought the impulse to storm over and defend her scribbled patterns. She had used runes gleaned from old scrolls, from the fortress library, from Rhezan's own recollections. If Sera wanted to threaten or belittle them all, let her. Nyra needed to focus on Rhezan's immediate condition.

She dipped a hand into her leather satchel and retrieved a small vial. The dull green liquid inside shimmered with a faint swirl of gold flecks. It was one of her more potent remedies for shock or magical backlash. She had never before tested it on a full-scale dragon. She muttered a silent prayer that Rhezan might find his way through the haze if she managed to coax enough of the potion into his mouth. The king offered a worried nod, watching as she carefully tilted Rhezan's snout to open a slight gap in the scaled jaw.

As she worked, Sera's irritated voice carried across the chamber. "I see incomplete lines. I see places where your incantation must have twisted. It is plain that too much blood might have aggravated the wards. Look at these deep gouges... the runes have been scorched. Were you out of your mind, cutting your palm so heavily?"

Nyra brushed hair away from her face. She wanted to retort, but she forced herself to remain calm. Another wave of raw emotion coiled in her chest. She fed Rhezan a small measure of potion, letting a few droplets slide down his throat. "One crisis at a time," she murmured.

Soon enough, Sera turned her attention to King Vorian, voicing criticisms about how the entire attempt had been handled. The king spoke in a low, measured tone that rose occasionally into sharper defense of Nyra's plan. Nyra caught the words "At least she tried," more than once. The privy councilors added harried nods, eager to maintain peace between the king and his returning ambassador.

Nyra listened with half an ear, cradling Rhezan's snout in her arms. The weight of his head was significant. Warm droplets from her cut palm dripped onto the scales, but she ignored the sting. She felt she had something to prove: that once he stirred, no one could question her devotion to ensuring his survival. He deserved better than being discarded as a lost cause by those who had never known the same measure of sacrifice.

A short time later, the conversation around her settled into uneasy silence. Every time Nyra glanced up, she found Sera's gaze fixed on her, cold and severe. Sera seemed furious that Nyra held Rhezan's life in her stained hands. That icy glare spoke of unyielding disapproval and an undercurrent of rivalry. The tension was so thick it nearly choked the air from the chamber.

Nyra returned her focus to Rhezan, placing a gentle kiss on the ridge above his brow. She swore she felt a small shift in his breathing. No movement in his limbs yet, but the breath was stronger, more stable. Relief flickered in her chest, even if it was fragile.

A final outburst came from Sera. "What else do you

plan to do, Healer, to revive him? If your potions fail, does this story just end here?"

Nyra swallowed her frustration. Tears stained her cheeks, but her words emerged steady. "This story will not end here," she promised. "Rhezan will wake. I will see to it, no matter how many spells or potions I must attempt."

Sera sniffed in disbelief. She eyed Nyra as if measuring her worth and finding it inadequate. Meanwhile, King Vorian signaled that he had heard enough for the moment. "Let us give Nyra space," he said. "We will not crowd the prince. He needs quiet."

Sera did not move at first. Only when the privy councilors touched her cloak lightly did she step back. She regarded Nyra with a look that mingled suspicion, contempt, and wounded pride. That look made Nyra's skin prickle. The woman's ire was so tangible that it seemed to crackle in the stale cavern air.

In that unspoken standoff, Nyra recognized a sharp truth: Sera would contest her at every turn. The ambassador's fury was personal, fueled by more than simple fear for Rhezan's safety. Nyra did not know the entire history between them, but she felt certain that Sera's hostility would only deepen.

From this moment on, from the way Sera looked at her like she was a bug to be crushed, Nyra knew the two women would be bitter enemies. She did not know how the ambassador's return to Varynth Hold would affect her fragile bond with Rhezan, but the challenge in Sera's glare promised unforgiving trials ahead.

CHAPTER

TWENTY

Nyra pressed her fingertips against a chilled cloth laid over Rhezan's forehead, her heart filled with relentless worry. Three weeks had passed since the failed ritual left him teetering in a realm of restless unconsciousness. Every day, she felt the cold stone of Varynth Hold press in on her, matching the icy dread that twisted inside her. She had tried anything and everything: gentle restorative potions, half-formed incantations, whispered pleas at his bedside when no one was looking. Yet for so long, Rhezan simply lay still, trapped behind his closed eyes.

She woke each morning determined to do better. On the first day after the ritual collapsed, she applied sweet-smelling salves enriched with windgrass and sunberry. She recalled how Rhezan once responded positively to her herbal mixtures. Her hands shook as she ground the ingredients together, but her resolve never wavered. When that failed to rouse him, she spent several sleepless nights consulting old grimoires, including her guarded blood-magic text. She discovered small spells rumored to spark life back into a dormant soul, though the pages offered no guarantee.

She made a minor cut along her palm on the tenth day, letting bright drops of her blood soak into a bowl of simmering moonleaf tea. She chanted quietly, glancing over the faint runes etched into the floor around Rhezan's bed. She felt a faint stirring at her magic's core, but no movement came from him. Each attempt was a sting of disappointment. Still, she pressed forward without hesitation.

On the sixteenth day, the fortress guard brought her news: the king had ordered the scouts to search for more Emberleaf along the far edges of the mountain slopes. Everyone was desperate for any lead that might help. The nights turned even colder after that, and Nyra sometimes felt her breath fog as she knelt by Rhezan's side in the cavern, reading quietly from a poetry collection. She told herself that maybe, if he heard her voice, he would decide to come back.

On the twenty-second day, just before dawn, Rhezan's eyelids finally fluttered open. The moment she saw his eyes move, she tensed in shock. She rushed to his side, forgetting in her excitement to be gentle, and collided with his foreleg. Despite the soreness in her shin, she cupped his scaled cheek, urging him not to slip away again. She had never felt relief so profound. His golden eyes held confusion, but they were open, and for the first time in weeks, he breathed in steady awareness. She stayed with him for hours, watching and waiting. He drifted in and out of consciousness, sometimes mumbling fragments she could not decipher. Yet the color and strength gradually returned to his scaled limbs and to that commanding aura she had grown used to.

His father, King Vorian, arrived not long after, nearly tripping with haste as he hurried into Rhezan's chamber. He sank to his knees beside Nyra, giving her a humble nod of gratitude. He pressed both hands against Rhezan's flank as he slumbered, overwhelmed to see his son rejoining the waking world.

Soon after, Sera and the privy councilors learned of Rhezan's recovery. Word spread that the prince was stirring, albeit weakened. Tension grew like a crack along the fortress walls, for no one knew what would be decided now that Rhezan had survived this brush with death. Had the ritual's failure drained him beyond the point of a cure? Or was there still hope?

The king announced that everyone crucial to Rhezan's fate would gather at sunset in the Great Hall to discuss next steps. By dusk, Nyra stood near the massive double doors, heart thrumming nervously. Servants lit torches and prepared a roaring hearth at the east end of the hall, for the night had arrived with a biting chill carried down from the mountaintops.

She followed two guards across the stone floor, mindful of the barrier that circled the center of the hall. Past that ring of tall pillars, Rhezan's form loomed, once more in his large draconic shape. Though he was still not at his full vigor, his presence was imposing enough to warrant the biggest room in the fortress. His obsidian scales caught the flicker of the torchlight, soaking it in as if aspiring to devour the entire chamber's glow.

Nyra lowered her head respectfully and moved closer. She wanted to stand by Rhezan's side, but the crowd of voices made it difficult to find an immediate path without stepping on shoes or boots. The hall was crowded. The king waited at the front of the dais, cloak draped regally over his shoulders. The privy councilors fidgeted near a polished wooden table, while Sera hovered to the left, arms crossed in front of her embroidered robe. Despite the hush of the hall, an unmistakable friction radiated from Sera's every measured breath.

Eventually, a herald banged his staff on the floor, calling the gathering to order. King Vorian addressed them with a subdued voice. He began by describing the ordeal of the past weeks, voice tight with gratitude that his son was alive. Then he gestured to Nyra.

"Nyra Vexlin," he said, wearing all the authority of a king but tempered with paternal warmth, "your perseverance these last weeks saved my son's life."

She stepped forward, pulses of apprehension dancing through her veins. "Your Majesty, I only did what I could. My greatest regret is that our ritual failed." Her eyes flicked toward Rhezan. She felt him watching her, studying the way her words faltered.

"It failed for now," the king amended, standing straighter. "But we must consider how to proceed. If we do nothing, Rhezan remains bound. We remain vulnerable to enemies waiting for a moment of weakness."

Councilor Harmond cleared his throat. "Your Majesty,

with all respect, we cannot ignore the fact that her blood-magic nearly cost Prince Rhezan his life. Are we certain we wish to try that again?"

Nyra's jaw tightened. She was tired, having spent weeks fighting for Rhezan to wake. Yet she understood their fear. She forced herself to stand tall. "The ritual indeed risked his life. It was a gamble we agreed to take," she said. "But the underlying power responded. We saw him cross the boundary between dragon and man. Something was working, only to be undone by factors I might have overlooked."

Sera's voice sliced through the gathering, cool and sharp. "Overlooked. That is a tame word for mortal danger," she remarked, stepping forward far enough that Nyra caught the silver lines of her robe swirling against the floor. "We have no desire to bury our prince in an early grave. Blood-magic is inherently unstable, and I continue to question why you are allowed to wield it at all."

Nyra's spine burned. She had no illusions about Sera's hostility. Their confrontation at the cave had etched Sera's distrust into every moment since. Still, Nyra lifted her chin and answered evenly, "Because your prince asked me to. He saturates my every thought, my every worry. Do not pretend I am here for any reason other than helping him."

Sera's glare flashed. "Helping him by nearly shredding his flesh from the inside? That was quite the demonstration of goodwill."

A low rumble filled the hall. Nyra realized it came from Rhezan, who shifted his wings, letting the torchlight ripple against his scales. Before the conversation could escalate, King Vorian raised a hand for silence. Then, with a grave nod, he turned once more to Nyra. "Tell us your insights, in as much detail as you can."

Nyra bent her head. "Certain aspects of the runes we used seemed to flicker erratically. That suggests our power supply was inconsistent. And I think we need more Emberleaf. Also, I suspect the fortress wards might have interfered with my incantations, siphoning away the energy at a critical moment."

She paused, meeting the watchful gaze of a stocky privy councilor. "If I am permitted to continue, I will realign the runes, confirm I have every necessary ingredient, and map out the fortress wards so they do not clash with the ritual. Then, when we attempt the ritual again, the risk might be better controlled."

She was acutely aware that she was sounding more confident than she felt. Inside, her heart dropped at the memory of Rhezan's final roar of agony. But she refused to let Sera see that vulnerability. She looked up at Rhezan, prepared to endure his verdict, or anyone else's.

For a moment, Rhezan remained silent in his great draconic shape. Then, with rumbling exhalation, he shifted himself across the hall. His massive foreclaws scraped sparks from the stone. Finally, his voice emerged, deeper and sharper than usual, though he aimed it not at Nyra, but across the floor to Sera.

He said, "You want me to remain like this forever? You left me once with no farewell. Now you expect me to trust your judgment about my curse?" His words echoed from high in the rafters.

Sera froze. Nyra saw an unguarded flicker of pain cross the ambassador's face, though it vanished behind a mask of composure. Sera lifted her chin. "I never asked you to trust me. I do not want you to die. That is the difference here. If there is another method to break your curse, we should find it. Without blood-magic."

"That is not your decision," Rhezan answered coldly. "You have no influence over me anymore." His wings rustled, and Nyra could feel the frustration coursing through him. "You cannot pretend to speak for my well-being if you stand here, sabotaging the only viable approach we have found. I trust Nyra, not you, and I will answer only to her counsel on this matter."

Nyra tried to hide the warmth that blossomed in her chest from his words. She had not expected him to be so direct. Sera's eyes glinted with a kind of wounded pride, and she shot Nyra a vicious look. Nyra could practically hear the silent accusation: interloper, meddler, unworthy.

King Vorian stepped in, voice calm but firm. "That is enough. Our time may be short. Our enemies watch us. If we linger in indecisiveness, we risk an open invitation to every hostile realm." He gestured for them to settle, though Rhezan's enormous shape continued to loom.

Sera inhaled a measured breath and squared her shoulders. "Indeed, we have enemies. Yet the only reason they have not stormed our gates is that they fear the might of a living dragon within these walls. If Rhezan becomes human again, what exactly will protect us from invasion?"

She addressed the king directly, ignoring Rhezan's

bristling posture. "He might be your son, but to our rivals, he is your ultimate weapon. A man in place of a dragon does not incite the same terror." Her gaze then drifted around the hall, meeting various councilors. "So I question whether lifting the curse so hastily is wise. Perhaps, if we find a safer method, or wait for better resources—"

Rhezan released a growl that vibrated through the floor. "You think I want to remain a dragon? Sera, you never understood the burden. Being seen solely as a weapon, even by those I once trusted."

He turned his massive head to look at King Vorian. "Father, we have only one immediate threat. You know who it is. Telandria has never recognized your sovereignty, cursed heir or not. I don't think even Sera's work as ambassador has changed their minds about us. They are not our allies. But if I reclaim my rightful place as heir, the other loyal realms will rally behind me. I must be human for them to see me as a ruler, not a monstrous curiosity. If we fail to show them a man with a claim to the throne, everyone will side with Telandria...and against us."

Telandria had always eyed the Drakareth northern territories with a hungry sort of patience. Once part of a shared empire, the two kingdoms had fought bitterly during the trade negotiations, and a war followed. When King Vorian won, Telandria had never truly accepted the borders that followed. King Vorian's ascent to the throne, backed by bloodline but not by consensus, only deepened the divide. The king of Telandria called him opportunist, not sovereign—his rule was cemented during the years before Rhezan's curse. For years, they claimed King

Vorian's throne should have passed through another line, one conveniently entwined with their own nobility.

Peace talks flared and faded like false dawns, and even Sera's diplomacy couldn't bridge a grudge rooted in old wars and older ambitions. Telandria didn't just reject Drakareth's sovereignty—they believed it was theirs to claim.

Nyra let out a shaky breath. His words confirmed that everything hinged upon forging a stronger magic that truly freed him. Her plan to realign wards and locate Emberleaf was all she had. If Sera managed to sway the king or the council that a gentler approach existed, Rhazan might remain cursed until war burst through Varynth Hold's gates.

Sera spun toward Rhezan, voice nearly trembling. "You are blinded by your desperation. When you topple back into unconsciousness, or when your body is twisted half to death, do not blame me for warning you."

Rhezan's roar of anger would have shaken the entire fortress if not for the king's sudden intervention. Vorian lifted both arms, voice booming. "Enough!" He let the echoes ring, ensuring every seat and corner of the hall remained silent. "I will not let internal squabbling tear us apart. The risk from outside grows every day. We will break the curse. Nyra, you will have all the assistance you require. Any who stands in your way answers to me."

Nyra's eyes stung with gratitude, mingling with a flood of tension. She bowed her head, whispering a brief acknowledgment. Still, she knew Sera's resentment would only fester. The ambassador's expression revealed open disapproval.

With forced calm, King Vorian cast a meaningful glance around the chamber. "The matter is settled. I name Nyra as the one with authority to continue her blood-magic if necessary to free my son. I want no more doubt sown on that front."

Sera's lips thinned into a stern line, but she did not wait to be addressed. "That is all well and good to proclaim," she said icily, turning to face Nyra, "But if this attempt fails, and our kingdom is overrun by enemies emboldened by the prince's downfall, you will be put to death as a threat to all the kingdoms for using your blood-magic."

TWENTY-ONE

Nyra stood in the Great Hall, scanning the vaulted ceilings as she tried to steady her breathing. It was still early morning, and the place lay hushed, free of courtiers and armed guards. Only the echo of her own footsteps followed her along the polished stone floor. She felt the weight of the fortress pressing in: looming tapestries, dark corners steeped in hidden whispers. Ordinarily, she would have welcomed such quiet. Today, the silence rattled her nerves.

She had agreed to meet Ambassador Sera here. The request had come by way of a steward who found Nyra just after breakfast. Sera insisted it was urgent. Nyra could guess why: the kingdom teetered on the edge of war, and the rumors of disastrous ritual attempt to cure Rhezan still lingered in every corridor and council meeting. She wondered if Sera simply wanted to gloat over that failure or if something darker was brewing. Either way, Nyra would not walk away from this conversation, no matter how tense.

At last, Sera's brisk footsteps announced her arrival. The ambassador entered from one of the side corridors, her richly embroidered cloak swishing across the stone. Although she was slender in build, the intensity in her posture made her seem taller. Without preamble, she advanced on Nyra, cold gray eyes locked in a determined stare.

"You came," Sera said. Her tone was clipped, as though she found courtesy a chore. She paused a few paces from Nyra, inhaled, then continued. "We need to talk, and we must do so away from the king and the others."

Nyra kept her spine straight, ignoring the flutter of tension at the base of her neck. "So I've heard."

Sera's eyes darted around the dim corners, verifying no eavesdroppers lurked behind a column or tapestry. Then her gaze settled fully on Nyra. "War is coming sooner than we feared," she said softly. "Every scout's report points to a gathering force at our borders. If what I've heard from my old post is correct, armies from more than one realm plan to strike once they confirm the prince is... incapacitated."

Nyra's heart twisted. She had sensed the building dread in the fortress. Yet hearing it stated so plainly sent a chill along her arms. "The prince is not incapacitated," she replied.

"Be that as it may," Sera said with a faint tighten of her lips, "the rumor of his weakness has spread. I have no illusion that a single show of flight will quiet all doubts. The enemy believes this kingdom to be unstable, and they will invade if they think victory is assured."

"And how," Nyra asked, trying to keep her voice from trembling, "am I involved in these rumors of war?"

Sera folded her arms over her chest, embroidered sleeves catching the muted torchlight. "Because your blood-magic is the fuse. If you continue seeking to break Rhezan's curse—especially in such reckless ways—you risk not only killing him but also weakening our wards, our fortress... everything." She took a step closer. "I need you to leave Varynth Hold. Renounce your blood-magic. Secure your future, before it is too late."

Nyra gasped. No matter what Sera's expression said, she remembered that fierce condemnation the woman had hurled at ther after he failed ritual. "You truly believe," Nyra managed, "that if I go home to my village, the war threat will vanish? That the realms circling us like vultures will stand down simply because I'm no longer here?"

Sera exhaled, exasperation and worry mingling in her gaze. "I do not promise the threat will vanish. I only say that if you renounce your practice"—her eyes flicked briefly to Nyra's palm, the faint scar from the blade she used to cut herself—"there may be a chance to broker peace. I still have political contacts in the other kingdoms. If you leave, if you swear never to use blood-magic again, the king might pardon you, and the other realms might see that we've stowed away the most dangerous element fueling this crisis."

"How convenient," Nyra said, biting back a surge of

anger. "You would see me vanish from the fortress, leaving Rhezan's curse unsolved."

Sera closed her eyes for a moment. "The prince's curse is not more important than the survival of this realm."

"You cannot expect me to accept that," Nyra said, voice rising before she forced it calmer. "This war threatened the kingdom long before I arrived. My presence here is to help—Rhezan, and the people at risk if the monarchy collapses. If we do not break the curse and restore him fully, your enemies might tear this land apart." She paused, aware of how her own resolve rang in her chest. "I will not abandon him."

The flicker of fear that crossed Sera's face told Nyra the conversation would only grow more heated. "I am offering you a chance to save your own life," Sera insisted. "We both know you stand on the edge of a blade. You used outlawed magic. You nearly killed the prince once. When these armies come—and they will—do you imagine the throne will protect you, or do you think the king will scapegoat the sorceress who dabbled in foul rites?"

Nyra's throat felt tight. She knew the risk. She understood that if she failed in her next attempt, or if enemies hammered down the gates, blaming the blood-mage might be an easy path for frightened nobles. "That does not matter," she said. "I will still try to free Rhezan."

Sera's lips pressed into a thin line. For a long moment, they stared at each other. Then Sera spoke, more softly, "Do you truly intend on risking beheading for a man who might not even survive the next attempt?"

Nyra's anger flared. "I do."

Silence swallowed them. Voices in the corridor beyond the hall hinted that servants approached, but Nyra heard no footsteps drawing closer. She half-expected Sera to press her advantage and threaten her again. Instead, the ambassador's gaze flickered with a faint sadness before she squared her shoulders.

"You are a fool," Sera said. "You do not see how quickly the tide can turn against you. Even now, the memories of my romance with Rhezan weigh on me." She paused, swallowing. "Yes, I once loved him. That was reality, before his curse and before I lost everything I thought we had. If your presence is the last wedge that drives him deeper into danger, so be it. But you cannot claim ignorance when this war arrives and devours you."

Nyra's fingers tightened around the edge of the nearest table. She forced herself to take a slow breath through her nose. "I am sorry you feel that way. But my decision stands. I will not leave him to face this alone."

Sera's mouth tilted near a sneer, but there was no further outburst. It felt as if the two of them had reached a final, irreversible impasse. Nyra's heart pounded, determined yet unsettled. She believed the words she had spoken. She refused to run. Knowing Sera had once been Rhezan's beloved did, however, stir a bitter ache within her—though she refused to let it show.

Before either of them could speak again, a new presence entered through the far doorway. The sound of claws scraping on polished stone, followed by the low rumble of breath, announced Rhezan's arrival. He was in a draconic form that managed to fit the hall: large but not at his maximum size. The black of his scales gleamed with an obsidian sheen, and his molten-gold eyes fixed on Sera with a disconcerting intensity.

"So this is how you plan to help?" His voice, edged with a draconic growl, resonated through the Great Hall. "You corner Nyra when no one else is here and attempt to coerce her into leaving?"

Nyra felt heat rush to her cheeks. She had not realized Rhezan might have heard. Sera, too, turned swiftly, her face tightening with fury or guilt. "It is not coercion. It is sense," Sera said tightly. "I am trying to protect her from the war that even the king cannot prevent."

Rhezan advanced another few feet, tail lashing behind him. Most of the time, he tried to appear calm in front of others, but Nyra saw the tension gripping his posture. "Protecting her," he repeated, voice low, "by telling her to run away from her vow to help me. You disgust me, Sera."

"These are harsh words," Sera said, bristling under his glare. "I do not ask her to run from everything, only from the gallows that might await her."

Rhezan snorted, puffs of smoke curling in the cold air. "If you genuinely cared for this kingdom, you would stand by the only person who can break my curse. You would not fill her head with empty promises about pardons and safety. The entire reason she was brought here was to fight for my cure."

Sera huffed, fists clenched at her sides. "It is not an empty promise. If she stops meddling in lethal magic, she might still negotiate with the other realms. They fear her power. If she sets it aside—"

"I am done." Rhezan's roar rumbled off the stone pillars, causing a few torch flames to flicker. "Your counsel is stale and self-serving." He turned his massive head to Nyra. "Are you well?" he asked, quieter.

Nyra nodded, exhaling the tension knotting her shoulders. "I am fine," she said, stepping closer to Rhezan. She tipped her head back, looking up at him. The anxious throb in her chest eased, replaced by the simple relief of seeing him there, protective and unwavering. She lifted a hand to his scaled face, letting her fingertips rest gently along the curve of his jaw. The texture of his scales, both smooth and impossibly tough, guided a tender warmth through her. He leaned slightly into her touch, and her heart twisted with gratitude.

Sera's posture stiffened, as if she found the sight of Nyra and Rhezan's closeness intolerable. "You truly believe you will both survive if she remains here?" she demanded. "If a legion of troops marches on Varynth Hold, do you expect them to be deterred by a half-cured prince and his renegade healer?"

Rhezan turned his gaze away from Nyra's face just long enough to stare down Sera. "I will do whatever it takes to protect this fortress, even if it means flying into their lines. But first and foremost, I will not permit you to poison Nyra's resolve with your fear."

Nyra slowly lowered her hand, but she stayed close to Rhezan's side. "Ambassador," she said, addressing Sera in a measured tone, "I will repeat once more: I will not leave. Whatever consequences come, be they war or condemnation for my blood-magic, I will face them. My place is here."

Sera's lips parted as though to argue, but words seemed to fail her. The set of her jaw revealed simmering anger, and perhaps an unspoken wound at seeing Rhezan stand so decidedly with someone else. At length, Sera let out a slow breath, nodding curtly. "Then you have made your choice," she said. "I hope you do not come to regret it."

She turned on her heel, cloak swirling behind her, and left by the same narrow corridor that had ushered her in. Her footsteps echoed a rapid staccato as she vanished into the fortress gloom. The Great Hall fell silent again, except for the muted hiss of the hearth fire at the far end. Nyra felt that same hush wrap around her, though her pulse still thundered.

Rhezan released a low rumble and bent his head down to her level, so his gold eyes all but filled her vision. "Are you sure about your decision?" he asked. His tone gripped her heart. "You heard her. If war comes, you might be spared if you leave now. Sera has been my father's favorite envoy. She could secure you a safe passage back to your home, if you like. If you wanted a new life somewhere else."

Nyra shook her head, stepping even closer. "I have a new life. It is here with you." She meant every word. She had never been more certain of anything. "Rhezan, I know you do not want me unnecessarily endangered. But I can't run away. Not after everything we've struggled through. I remain your healer." Her voice softened. "I am staying."

THE STORY CONTINES

The story continues in book two, *The Dragon's Bargain*, coming soon to Amazon.

EXCEPT FROM THE DRAGON'S BARGAIN

CHAPTER ONE

Nyra found the library of Varynth Hold even colder than she remembered. The tall windows admitted thin shafts of grayish light, barely enough to see the dust dancing in the air. It had been three weeks since the dreadful day the ritual to lift the curse from Prince Rhezan had failed. The prince had briefly been human again for a few breathtaking and heartbreaking moments, only to become a dragon again within seconds. To be fair, the exercise wasn't completely failure, it simply didn't completely work. Nyra could argue about the semantics of it all for hours but two facts remained. Fact 1: Rhezan had been human, which proved it was possible. Fact 2: Not being able to remain human meant there was something wrong with the ritual itself.

Varynth Hold, the castle fortress King Vorian and his son called home, still echoed with the tense undercurrent, and there was little doubt in Nyra's mind that the magic that had gone awry still lingered. It was an odd place. The runes carved into the stone walls of the castle, and deeper still, into the mountain caves it was built into, had absorbed arcane energy for centuries, drawing power from every spell cast by those who once lived there. Mages and healers could sometimes draw upon that ancient magic. Other times, if the castle's old magic felt temperamental, it could block anyone from tapping into that power at all. Nyra just had to figure out whether she didn't have the right keys to let her touch that magic, or if the magic of Varynth Hall was actively blocking her.

The library smelled of stale parchment and tallow candles. The scent put her briefly at ease, reminding her of simpler nights in her village cottage, where reading by lamplight held no deadly consequences. She arranged the arcane textbooks she had pulled off the shelves to her right, selected one and opened it in front of her. She arranged her battered notebook, quill, and inkpot where it was comfortable for her to take notes. It promised to be another long day of trying to crack the code of the ritual to find out where it had gone wrong.

The winds howled outside and if Nyla didn't know any better and from the drafts blowing into the room, she would have sworn that every stained glass window in the room didn't exist at all. Nyra pulled a thick shawl more tightly around her shoulders and crossed it over her chest. sShe tucked the ends of it into her belt to keep it from slipping loose. She also wore fingerless wool gloves that were supposed to help keep her hands warm as she wrote, but were quite ineffective. Still, the ache in her bones from the cold was nothing compared to the ache in her heart from letting everyone down, especially Rhezan.

She'd tried to stop punishing herself with the memory of the prince's pained roar when his body twisted as she spoke the incantation, and the helpless panic in her heart as his body rejected the spell meant to heal it and, instead, only allowed him a brief respite from his dragon's body. Nyra breathed in slowly, remembering how he'd been unconscious for days after, and how weak he was once he woke. She had refused to leave his side until he was healed. Even when Sera tried to get her to leave, adamant that performing ritual again would destroy them both, she had refused to leave. Her decision was absolute, shaped by a frightening mix of guilt, compassion, and something else she was afraid to admit—the emotional attachment she now shared with Prince Rhezan, and she was sure he felt it, too.

Nyra touched the faint wound on her right palm. Though the cut had healed, she still felt a phantom sting when she thought of how she had spilled her own blood to fuel the ritual. The memory twisted her heart, but she refused to let that weakness hold her back from trying again. Despite the uneasy atmosphere, with castle staff eyeing her warily everywhere she went, she wouldn't give up. Saying the castle had become her second home would have been a stretch: she kept to these secluded shelves, poring over anything that might illuminate the path forward.

She focused on the book in front of her, and read a passage on The Lament of Wyrmkin, which chronicled the history of the only other human-to-dragon transformation that Nyra had found in the dozens of books and scrolls of parchment she'd read. According to its author, a mage called Alessandra who reportedly cast the spell, there were two types of dragon transformations: full and partial. The full transformations, like Rhezan's, were supposed to be permanent or, at the very least, nobody had tried to reverse the spell to restore someone cursed to be a dragon to human again. The partial transformations seemed to be the type that allowed for intentional shifting from one form to another, if the ritual were performed in a controlled, precise manner.

Well, of course, rituals were supposed to be controlled and precise. Who would want a wild and uncontrolled spell that might lash out in unexpected ways, unravel your intentions, or worse—turn on you entirely? She frowned at the sloppy script. The entire account was riddled with more questions than answers, especially about the lasting power of half-shifts.

Nyra marked the section with a bookmark, and thumbed through the pages until she came across a ritual purporting to be a bridge between joining mortal flesh to other creature forms, specifically the scaled kind of creatures. The passage warned that in-between forms—so-called shifter spells—were inherently unstable without an anchor. No matter the will behind it, the magic would eventually seize control, tearing through muscle and bone to drag the body back to its dominant shape. Human or creature, it didn't matter. The shift would break before it bent.

Nyra exhaled, frustration running hot through her veins. Which answer was the right one? On one hand, it seemed both permanent and temporary transformations were possible—her failed attempt notwithstanding—and, on the other, anything but a permanent shift was doomed to fail at some point.

Rubbing her eyes, Nyra reminded herself that she had seen Rhezan flicker into and out of his human shape. His scaled face and body had given way to that of a man, and a damn handsome one, too. Yes, the ritual had nearly cost him his life, and he'd been unconscious for days, but it had also proven that a glimmer of hope existed. It was a flimsy sort of proof, one that could indicate either the curse could be lifted completely or could be partially lifted. She just had to figure out how to cast the ritual. She stopped a moment and sighed. It wasn't all she had to figure out. She must also ask Rhezan what he could live with if a full, permanent transformation wasn't possible. The shift was excruciatingly painful for him

She read for another long stretch, letting the hush of the library settle around her like a quilt. Aside from the occasional footsteps in the corridor, only the soft crackle of the fire in the grate made any sound. She never knew when Sera might appear, wearing the same disapproving look that had twisted her sour face for weeks. Then again, maybe that sourness was specifically reserved for her, which Nyra conceded was a distinct possibility.

The cold winds had nothing on Sera's personality. Nyra had once marvelled that there weren't icicles hanging from the woman's nose, so cold was her personality. She was graceful, sure. And beautiful. And had a body that had most of the men in the castle undressing with their eyes. But she was also cunning and, more than once, she overheard conversations—or was told second hand about them by her guards—about Sera forging alliances with anyone who would listen to her warnings about the dangers of Nyra's blood-magic.

Nyra felt the tension building. Aside from Rhezan and the king, only Thomas and the few guards assigned to her offered any warmth and companionship. Everyone else went stiff whenever she came close or tried to speak, as if they were afraid her blood-magic might explode out of her at any minute. The king's privy councilors did use polite, if not friendly, tones when speaking to her, but she still saw the wariness in their eyes. The entire castle seemed to brace itself, suspecting her next attempt at lifting the curse might be as disastrous as the first.

She peered down at a curling corner of parchment. She recalled Sera's sneering remark that if Nyra continued with her forbidden magic, she would be the first to face condemnation in the event of war. It still burned, stirring equal parts bitterness and nervous resolve to prove the woman wrong. She'd chosen to stay to help Rhezan, and no matter how much the threat of imprisonment—or even death—hung over her if the king changed his mind about her using outlawed blood-magic, her decision was made. She'd given her word, and that promise held.

She searched for anything that might offer clarity on what to try next. She found reference to a reinforcement incantation, something she'd read about, but had never done herself. A reinforcement incantation wasn't the main invocation used to cast a spell or lift a curse, it was used to augment the spell that did. In the case of lifting the dragon curse on Rhezan, the additional incantation might give his body time to adapt to the enormous surge of magic going through him, to learn how to let the magic in without it tearing him apart.

If cast with care, it could offer a fragile kind of balance, enough to keep Rhezan from slipping between forms too quickly or losing control. But it was tricky work. Push too hard, and you risked sealing the wrong shape. Go too soft, and the magic snapped like wet string.

Nyra tapped the table with her fingers, thinking it through, then took more notes. A partial fix might still cause pain but if it gave Rhezan even a little more control, allowed him to shift at will, then he might be willing to try it despite the pain.

She let out a shaky breath. Truth didn't follow clean lines. Love, loyalty, and fear had tangled itself into the magic embedded in the castle and within her soul. And no book, no matter how ancient or wise, could untangle what she felt.

A soft scraping sound startled her from her thoughts. She looked up. The library door nudged open, and Rhezan, in his smaller dragon shape, slipped inside. The sight of his obsidian scales reflecting the candlelight sent a strange mix of relief and longing coursing through her. She forced her breathing to remain steady while he took a few steps forward. Even in his reduced size, he towered over the piles of books on her table, each clawed footfall gentle on the library's polished floor. He said nothing for a moment.

"Rhezan," she greeted him, "you look like you're feeling better."

Telling if a dragon is feeling poorly is different than with humans. With a person, a sickly pasty pallor is usually a dead giveaway that they're not at top form. With dragons, it's the eyes. The glow dims first—a subtle fading, like embers cooling beneath ash. Then the sharpness goes. A healthy dragon's eyes track everything, alert and calculating. But when they're unwell, that fire dulls. The gaze goes glassy, slow to focus, sometimes flickering with pain they won't admit. If you know them well, you'll see it before anything else: the brightness is gone, and in its place is something quieter. Heavy. Like they're holding themselves together by instinct alone. Rhezan's eyes looked pained.

She gestured to the space beside her, where a sturdy visitor's chair sat untouched. Of course, Rhezan couldn't use it. Instead, he settled beside the table in a half-crouch, folding his legs beneath him and angling his wings carefully so they wouldn't brush the stained-glass lamp. He dipped his head to study her notes, the gold in his eyes caught the lamplight with a soft, otherworldly glow. She noticed the slight tilt of his head—a signal she'd come to recognize as quiet attentiveness. Her chest tightened.

"Have you found anything yet?" he asked.

"I did, but the information is quite contradictory. One passage says both temporary and permanent transformations are possible, but another says temporary shifts, human one moment and dragon the next, cannot be maintained." She tried to keep the frustration out of her voice. His mood was easily affected these days, no surprise there. He'd experienced so much disappointment he'd begun to expect it as status quo.

He responded with a low rumble, a sound that usually meant acknowledgment. She tried to interpret the nuance in it: a soft acceptance that the research was complicated, perhaps. Slowly, she turned a page in her battered notebook. Candlelight danced across the reinforcement incantation as she explained it to him. She traced the faint lines of runes she'd drawn, explaining how they could be woven into the existing wards so they could work together.

"So, a reinforcement incantation is more like a scaffold than the cure itself. Does it hurt?"

Nyra's hand stilled on the page. The question came so quietly, so simply—but it struck her like a blade between the ribs. There was no flinch in his voice, no dread. Just the weary resignation of someone who had learned to expect pain as part of living. Her throat tightened. He didn't even ask if it would work. Only if it would hurt.

She looked up at him, and her heart cracked under the weight of what he wasn't saying. That he would endure it. That he already had. That maybe, deep down, he didn't believe there could be a version of himself that didn't hurt.

Nyra forced a breath, steadying her voice before she answered. "If it's anything like the first time, yes, it will hurt. But if the ritual works, will the pain be worth it?"

He tilted his head, exhaling gently so he would not

exhale flame by accident. She noticed his posture shift, as though a fleeting spark of caution or hope stirred within him, and then she had the answer to the question, perhaps the most important one. "Yes. It would be worth it."

Nyra drew her candle closer so he could see the ritual she was writing in her notebook more clearly. Her voice grew quieter. "I have never tried a ritual quite like this. It will require my blood again to link the runes to everything in the ritual, including the reinforcement incantation. We will strengthen the shape you choose to hold so your intentions in those moments are crucial to lift the curse."

Rhezan stretched his wings, letting out a low huff that served as a soft expression of agreement or at least willingness to consider. She dared a small smile. For the first time in weeks, she sensed a flicker of optimism rather than a crushing sense of dread. Even the gloom of the library felt a shade lighter as she turned back to her notes.

"If I tell you something, do you promise not to panic?" he asked.

The question was so strange, so unlike Rhezan that she stopped writing mid-sentence. She pinned him with a stare. "No, I can't promise something like that without knowing what this something is."

"Then forget I said any—"

"No, I can't forget. You already spoke the words." Sometimes, Rhezan could be a complete idiot. "It's already out there, and I'm going to keep prodding you until you crack, so you might as well just tell me."

He didn't meet her eyes. Instead, he tilted his head

slightly away, gaze fixed somewhere just beyond her shoulder. His tail gave a slow, agitated flick across the floor.

"I don't want to make things worse," he muttered, almost too low for her to catch.

Nyra waited.

His throat worked in a swallow, and when he finally looked at her, there was a flicker of vulnerability behind the gold. Something unsteady. Something unguarded. His wings folded in tight then, a protective gesture. Not angry. Just... bracing.

"I still feel it," he said, voice low. "Your blood-magic. It's still inside me."

Nyra froze. Her quill hovered above the page, the ink bleeding onto one spot. "What do you mean, you feel it?"

He shifted his weight, claws scraping softly against stone. "It's like... heat, under my skin. Not pain, exactly. But it pulses sometimes, especially when the castle's wards shift. It's like something wakes up in me. And it's yours. I know it."

Nyra set the quill down. "That's not... That shouldn't be possible." Her voice faltered and she frowned, her eyes scanning his face, searching. "Blood-magic doesn't linger. Not like that. It's supposed to bind, or activate, or heal, and then fade."

He looked at her then, and her breath caught. His eyes had always glowed, but now something inside them shimmered, and it was familiar and strange all at once. The color was deeper, as though her magic had left behind a trace of memory, a thread still woven into him.

"What does it feel like now? Right this second."

Rhezan shut his eyes. "Warm. But wrong. It hums when I breathe wrong. Or when I'm completely still."

Nyra let her hand hover near his chest, not touching, just holding space. "Okay, I never anticipated this. But with my blood-magic still inside you, and the fact you've already shifted to human once, however briefly, you might be able to do it again. And if I'm not with you when it happens, you need a way to control it."

"How am I supposed to do that?" His tone was immediately sharp and challenging. "I have no clue what I'm doing."

He had a point. She didn't know what she was doing either, not completely, anyway. The only thing she had to fall back on, at this point, was a mundane, non-magical remedy for managing stress.

"Breathe with me."

"What?"

"Follow my lead. Every breath I take, you do the same."

"How is that supposed to help?"

"It's an old practice. It's just meant to help you stay calm."

He hesitated. "I remember how. I try. But it's harder now."

"That's okay," she said. She had no precedent for this, no record in any grimoire that warned what to do when your blood-magic *stayed* in someone else's body. But she could see how tightly he held himself, the tension carved into every joint, every line of his face. He needed grounding. And if nothing else, she could give him that.

"Match me," she said gently. "In through your nose... slowly. Four heartbeats."

She inhaled, deliberately slow, and watched as his chest rose unevenly.

"Good. Now hold it for four counts."

His wings twitched, but he did it.

"And now, in four counts, slowly let it out through your mouth."

They repeated the pattern. Again. And again.

The glow in his eyes dimmed just a little, shifting from strain to something steadier.

"Feel better?" she asked.

He considered her for a moment, clearly pondering whether he did, in fact, feel better. "I don't feel worse. I think it helped a little."

"Okay, so if you feel like you might shift when you don't want to, before you start panicking, try the breathing exercise."

"And if it doesn't work?"

"Fair question," she conceded. "In that case, I have a feeling the entire castle will know about it."

She watched him for a minute or two. His eyes were closed and he kept breathing, and somewhere inside her she felt what he was talking about. They were connected. She'd felt him, along with the magic energy humming in the walls, the first few nights she was in the castle. Now, he seemed to feel it even more strongly than she had. She'd have to keep her eyes on that situation.

"I'm not sure what's happening," Nyra admitted. "But I think... whatever part of my magic stayed behind, it's responding to something inside you. It could be a good thing. We just have to keep it under control."

His gaze met hers—less wild now, more focused. "And keep breathing."

Nyra smiled, though her chest ached. "Right. And keep breathing."

OTHER FLORID ROMANCE BOOKS

To be notified of new releases and special promotions from Florid Romance, please join our email list:

https://floridromance.lmbpn.com/about/sign-up-for-our-newsletter/

For a complete list of books published by Florid Romance please visit our website:

https://floridromance.lmbpn.com/

BOOKS BY RIVER TATUM

The Dating Diary
One Is Too Many BF's (Book 1)
Two Many Choices (Book 2)
Three is A Crowd (Book 3)
Four Is a Disaster (Book 4)

<u>The Firebound Chronicles</u>
Forged in Flame (Book 1)
Bound By Flame and Illusion (Book 2)
Crowned in Flame and Oath (Book 3)

<u>Vows in Magic and Steel</u>
Duty Bound (Book 1)
Hearts in Conflict (Book 2)
Unbreakable Vows (Book 3)

<u>Sorcery and Secrets</u>
Sabotage (Book 1)

Suspicion (Book 2)
Seduction (Book 3)

Love on the MerChain Express
Route of Secrets (Book 1)
Merchant's Gambit (Book 2)
Without Illusions (Book 3)

The Dreamweaver's Pact
Whispering Dreams (Book 1)
Shattered Nightmares (Book 2)
Dawn Awakening (Book 3)

The Cursed Worm Court
The Healer and The Dragon (Book 1)
The Dragon's Bargain (Book 2)

BOOKS BY MICHAEL ANDERLE

Connect with Michael Anderle

Connect with Michael Anderle

Website: http://lmbpn.com

Email List: https://michael.beehiiv.com/

https://www.facebook.com/LMBPNPublishing

https://twitter.com/MichaelAnderle

https://www.instagram.com/lmbpn_publishing/

https://www.bookbub.com/authors/michael-anderle

www.ingramcontent.com/pod-product-compliance
Lightning Source LLC
Chambersburg PA
CBHW032238310726
48973CB00008B/2197